Three soldiers had been standing at the far end of the corridor. When the shooting had erupted, one of them opened the door to the nearest cell to take cover. Colon and Livingston took cover behind a wall; no sooner had they done so than one of the soldiers came flying back into the corridor, his hands clutching his throat, blood seeping between his fingers. A second man followed, a diagonal slash across his chest. There were sounds of a struggle; after a moment the third man fell out holding his side. Weyers stormed after him, punching the wounded man hard in the face. There was an explosion of blood and the German fell back.

The men then hurried to the far side of the prison. In one of the cells they found a heap that was barely human. They guessed it was Barker. Weyers gathered him gently in his arms. In the last cell, Livingston found Delphine. She was naked and sobbing, crouched in a pool of dirt and dark blood.

There was no doubt in his mind that she hadn't betrayed them. Which meant that somewhere, here or at home, there was still a traitor at large.

Perhaps, he had to admit, even in the Force Five team itself.

FORCE FIVE

DESTINATION: ALGIERS

Jeff Rovin

LYNX BOOKS

New York

DESTINATION: ALGIERS

ISBN: 1-55802-164-7

First Printing/February 1989

This book is published by Lynx Books, a division of Lynx Communications, Inc., 41 Madison Avenue, New York, New York, 10010. The name ''Lynx'' together with the logotype consisting of a stylized head of a lynx is a trademark of Lynx Communications, Inc.

Printed in the United States of America

0 9 8 7 6 5 4 3 2 1

FORCE
FIVE

Prologue

"I appreciate your position, General Marshall. Now you must appreciate *mine*."

General Sir Archibald Wavell moved his hands across his face, then gazed at the maps and documents spread before him.

"As I've said many times, if we don't strike at Rommel, hit him hard and hit him soon, he will be too well entrenched to be driven from North Africa. It's the reason Mr. Churchill proposed Operation Gymnast when America first got into this. It's the reason that we propose it again."

President Roosevelt's chief of staff, General George C. Marshall, looked down at his own set of maps. He, too, was tired, more tired than he'd been since Pearl Harbor. It had taken an exhausting eight months getting the U.S. military ready for mobilization in Europe. Now that that was done, the Americans and British couldn't agree on where to launch their first cooperative strike.

Marshall folded his leathery hands. He looked from Wavell to the Englishman's two colleagues. "Believe me, General, after nine hours in this room, I appreciate your concerns about Rommel.

But we need a certain victory to fire up morale. What my staff and I have suggested, an assault on the French channel coast, would not only catch the Germans off guard and rouse French resistance. It's something tangible, something that would capture the imagination of the American public and its servicemen.''

"It would also please Stalin if you were to do that—open a second front in Europe to take pressure off the Russians," Wavell said. "But may I remind you, this is the very same Stalin who made peace with Hitler and then sat on his hands while the Luftwaffe bombed the *hell* out of us! At least Mr. Roosevelt sent us arms. Stalin did *nothing!*"

"And are you looking to punish the Russians or reinforce the Eighth Army?"

"*I'm looking to win the bloody war!* I remind you again, sir, that if Rommel succeeds in getting as far east as El Alamein, the road to Alexandria and the Suez Canal will be his. If Suez falls, there is *nowhere* in the Mediterranean or Arabian Seas that will be inaccessible to the enemy. And if they gain access to the Middle Eastern oil fields . . .''

Wavell didn't finish. He sat back slowly and slapped his pockets in search of a cigarette. One of Marshall's four aides handed him a Lucky. The Englishman looked with open displeasure at the American brand, then reluctantly lit it.

Marshall stared at his colleague. Wavell's points about North Africa could not be ignored. But the Allies had been fighting together for all of 1942, and they'd suffered heavy losses in the Philippines, the Bataan Peninsula, and Corregidor. Wavell himself had taken a vicious beating in Burma. A defeat in the desert would be disastrous, whereas a successful if less significant landing in

France, on smooth, defensible terrain, would provide a much-needed boost in morale.

Still, Marshall knew that wars were not won by playing sure bets, and he turned to a detailed map of North Africa hanging from the wall of the Pentagon situation room.

"Something just occurred to me. Suppose we were to agree to a North African offensive in which the Americans take part—but as a separate entity. Let us have a victory, on our own, while we also take some of the pressure off your men."

Wavell blew several quick puffs on his cigarette, then ground it out. "You talk as though victory were mine to give."

"In a way, it is." Marshall picked up a pencil and pointed to the map. "Consider: three landings along the coast—Algiers, Oran, and Casablanca. The Germans run Algeria through the puppet French government, and are all over Algiers and Oran. But Casablanca is still up for grabs . . . and I've got an ambitious major general, Patton, who's been itching to storm something somewhere. I'll put him in charge of an all-American landing there, and give you men to support *your* boys as they take Algiers and Oran. Afterwards, all three task forces can link up and move against Rommel."

Wavell studied the map. "Casablanca should be easy enough, but there's a huge aerodrome outside of Algiers. German air cover will hurt us there and in Oran."

"Not if we hurt it first. Right before the landings, we'll send in a team—also American and British—to do as much damage as possible. Even if the Germans realize what we're up to, it'll be too late for them to bring in reinforcements."

Wavell considered the proposal, then his mouth

twisted into a faint smile. "I like it, General. I like it very much. And I believe Mr. Churchill will be amenable to your plan."

Marshall seemed relieved. "And I'm sure the president will accept. Which leaves the matter of the advance team. I assume you've already got people in the area who can do some groundwork."

Wavell nodded.

"Good. While they reconnoiter, we can put the word through channels here and abroad that we need a crack team to go in and do the dirty work. I'll get things moving on this end; you start looking on yours." Marshall grinned. "There is one thing, though, General."

Wavell's expression grew wary.

"Operation Gymnast is a damn lousy name for a military operation. Can you think of anything else?"

Wavell's smile returned. "Well—that *is* a problem." He thought for a moment. "In keeping with America's tendency to do things in a big way, might I suggest . . . Super-Gymnast?"

"Frankly, it's the Gymnast part that I find uninspired."

"I see." Wavell bowed slightly. "On that, General, I defer entirely to you."

As the men left the room, Marshall happened to notice a framed picture of the Statue of Liberty in the corridor.

He looked at the light she held aloft and smiled.

"Torch," he said under his breath. "Operation Torch."

Chapter One

Private Ernesto Colon's dark eyes narrowed. He felt it coming; he always did.

It wasn't just the sudden quiet in the locker room. The short, taut man felt a chill on the back of his neck whenever trouble was near, and he was never wrong about it. Not back home in the slums; not in four years at Duquesne; and not now, at Fort Benning.

"Excuse me, soldier. I'd like to see you outside."

The gruff voice was followed by a hard tap on his shoulder. Colon continued facing his locker. He turned the game ball over in his hands. His own raspy voice was barely above a whisper. "You're seein' me here. What do you want?"

"I want to settle a score, hotshot. You played New York dirty with a friend of mine."

Colon ran his thumb along the seams. "Which friend was that?"

"Barry Kaplan. Last night, at the PX."

Colon scowled. *That* loudmouth. The sawbones who'd driven in from Fort Bragg for the game. "Your friend was shootin' off his yap about how Americans have no business goin' to fight in a foreign war. All I did was ask him if he'd fight in an American war. When he said yes, I started one."

"It's my understanding, *Private*, that your job is to defend citizens' rights to free speech, not try and restrict them. Isn't that correct?"

Colon turned now. The man before him was a head taller and barrel-chested. The private frowned when he saw that the man was a captain.

He started to turn back. The man tapped him again, this time in the shoulder blade.

"I asked you something, Private."

Over his shoulder, Colon said, "Yes, sir. Free speech. But if that applies to his flappin' gums, then it also applies to my knuckles. Sir."

Several of Colon's teammates coughed, and feet stamped lightly in a show of support.

The captain removed his jacket.

"You want to fight Americans, dogface? That's fine with me. Only let's see how you do with someone a little more physical than Kaplan."

"Thank you, sir, but I must decline. If I slug a superior officer, you win even if you lose."

"Are you chicken, Private?"

Colon squeezed the ball hard. "No, sir. But I've spent enough time in the cooler this month."

"This isn't army business, Colon, it's just you and me, man to man. You men"—he faced the others—"you're witnesses. This man will not be brought up on charges for anything he does during—"

The captain gasped, gurgled, then doubled over. Colon drove the football into his groin a second time; the officer stumbled back, fell over the bench, and landed against a locker. He slumped to the floor, moaning, his hands on his crotch.

The private stepped over, grabbed him by the tie. "Two things, Captain. First, no one tells me we shouldn't be fightin' Hitler a few weeks before my platoon ships out. Second, what I did wasn't New York dirty. New York dirty is a shiv or a .22. I hit your asshole friend with a ketchup bottle." He headed back to his locker. "Usin' what's handy—that's *Pittsburgh* dirty. Sir."

Returning to his locker, Colon undressed and headed for the shower. The room was warm again, and he allowed himself a smile.

Company Sergeant Major Kenneth Ogan stood by the window of the small room. His hands were clasped tightly behind his back, his blue eyes focused on something beyond the rows of barracks, beyond the distant Georgia hills.

On a crowded pub in Kensington.

On the rugged face of Harold Barker as the two of them shook hands for the last time, just before Barker was to be sent via Turkey to Algiers.

"Sons of bitches."

Colonel Donald LaJoie looked up from the dossier. "Excuse me?"

Ogan turned. "Sir?"

"You said something."

"Did I? I'm sorry. Must have been thinking aloud."

The colonel sipped a Coke. "Tough to relax, isn't it? My counterpart in London tells me you're one of the most fanatic workers he's ever met."

"We all do our part, sir."

The colonel shook his head. "No, you guys have been putting in overtime, mostly because of us. All this isolationist crap. What did Hitler have to do to get our attention, bugger Lady Liberty?"

The intercom buzzed and LaJoie leaned toward it. "Yes?"

"Private Colon to see you, sir."

"Thank you, Franklin. Have him wait." The colonel picked up the folder and rose. "Are you sure you don't want to glance at this? You may have second thoughts."

"I'm sure, sir. It wouldn't matter anyway, not this late in the game."

The colonel shrugged and asked his aide to send the soldier in.

Ogan turned toward the door. *No, it doesn't matter who walks in,* he thought. He'd flown over from London to get bodies. Good bodies, self-sufficient ones. From what he'd heard, Colon seemed to fill the bill. Still, he prayed that the private was more than just a pair of fists without the brains to know when to use them.

The door opened and a small, well-built man strode in. He saluted smartly, and though he faced the colonel his eyes were on Ogan.

LaJoie returned the salute. "At ease," he said, then sat on the edge of his desk. "First of all, Private, I want to congratulate you on a terrific game yesterday. It feels good to beat Bragg for a change. If it weren't for your two TDs, we never could have done it."

"Thank you, sir, but it really was a team effort."

Ogan perked up. He liked the sound of that.

"Bull," said the colonel. "I believe in giving credit where credit is due, just as I believe in putting the screws to gold brickers. You're the guy who dodged the tackles and ran the ball in, and you deserve the credit." His eyes narrowed. "Just like you're the guy I *should* ream out for knocking Captain Marrin on his keester."

Colon shifted uneasily.

"But I'm not going to do that, Colon. Marrin's a stuffed shirt, so we'll call it an extra point and let it go at that." LaJoie took a swig of Coke. "But this *is* the fifth fight you've had in the two months you've been here. How much KP have you pulled so far?"

"Nine days' worth, sir."

"And how many days in the stockade?"

"Two, sir."

LaJoie's brow furrowed and he glanced at the papers behind him. "Your file says four."

"Yes, sir. But you said here, sir. I got those other two days for fighting on the bus from Atlanta."

LaJoie frowned. "Tell me, Colon. How many more American soldiers do you expect to fight before we turn you loose on the Nazis?"

The private glanced at Ogan, who was watching him sternly. "I don't know, sir. I try to mind my own business, but things just seem to . . . happen."

"Things." LaJoie flipped open the file. "Like breaking the cook's nose at mess."

"He said his sausages weren't greasy enough for spics—"

"And hitting your bunk mate."

"He stole some letters from my dad and hid—"

"That'll *do*, Private! This is for the sergeant major's benefit, not yours."

Colon shot a questioning look at Ogan. The Englishman stepped forward. "What the colonel means, Private Colon, is that you won't be going overseas with your regiment. You'll be leaving with me at 0900 hours."

"With you?"

"You've been seconded to me for a job which requires a man of your particular talents—a tough team player who isn't afraid to be on his own, if need be. For security reasons, I can't tell you what our assignment is; you won't be briefed until we're all together in London. Suffice it to say that the

lives of thousands of men will depend upon what
we do over the next two weeks."

Ogan regarded Colon carefully. When he'd said
the young man wouldn't be going overseas, something in him seemed to die for a moment. Now
there was a glint in the American's dark eyes.
Ogan was glad to see it.

Colonel LaJoie finished his Coke. "It's done, Private. You'll continue at full pay, and there will be
other considerations when you return. I want you
to understand just how important this is."

"I understand, sir."

LaJoie studied Colon's dark eyes. "I'm not sure
you do. No matter what Sergeant Major Ogan
asks, no matter how much anyone rubs you the
wrong way, insubordination will not be tolerated.
And I'm not just talking about the stockade if you
screw up, Colon. We'll hit you with the book, and
then some."

"I understand, sir."

The soldier was dismissed and told to report
back to the colonel's office in an hour. Turning,
Ogan looked out the window and stared, once
again, into that faraway pub where he'd last seen
Barker.

It was July 1939. He and Barker were about to
go their separate ways, and reminiscences came
easily. About growing up. About boxing. About
youthful loves and enemies. Ogan's wife Cindy had
joined them, and for the first time Barker admitted he'd encouraged his sister and his best friend
to wed not just for their own happiness, but so
the three of them would always be close.

There were tears, laughter, and a promise to
meet again when Hitler was just a memory.

Ogan took a long, tremulous breath. He'd lost
friends in the war, and he mourned them, yet none

was Harold Barker. When Barker disappeared in Algiers, when reconnoitering at the aerodrome, Ogan had been pulled from his post at a temporary prison camp in Coventry for British soldiers. Since then, each second that had passed tortured him with the fear that he might be too late. And it hurt not to be able to tell his wife where he was going, or that her brother was missing. They had always shared everything, but it was better for Cindy, and for the orphanage where she worked, if she didn't have to worry.

At least now he had his team—a team with balls. Colon. Lambert. Weyers. Livingston—especially Livingston. Ogan didn't know whether they'd be in time to save Barker, but he was certain of two things: that the German war machine in Algiers would be made to suffer, and that whoever had leaked word of Barker's mission to the Nazis would suffer even more.

Sergeant Clayton Livingston stared from the open door of the Dakota, watching the hum of activity as the plane was supplied for its transatlantic journey.

He smelled the high-octane aviation fuel; smelled and remembered . . .

Smells and music. Nothing else brought back the past so vividly. Whenever he heard Artie Shaw records, he was back with Anna. Whenever he was at an airfield, the smells took him back to Spain. To France.

To hell.

Still, he told himself, *it was better to reign in hell than to serve behind a desk*.

Livingston shielded his eyes as a jeep rounded the hangar and came bouncing across the field. He

recognized Ogan in the backseat. The man beside
him had to be Colon.

Ernesto Colon. Son of a steel worker, Major
Maher had told him. All-City halfback. Football
scholarship to Duquesne. A brawler.

The jeep screeched to a stop beside the plane.
Ogan snatched his portfolio from the front seat
and hopped out; Colon grabbed his duffel bag and
emerged more slowly.

Livingston had promised Maher he wouldn't an-
tagonize Colon. He was the only other American
on the team, and the army wanted them to make
a good impression on the Brits. Besides, after
spending five months at Fort Custer in Michigan,
Livingston would have joined a regiment of Co-
lons just to get away from the base. Scheduling
inoculations, running films on venereal disease,
giving IQ tests before putting new recruits on
trains bound for Camp Wheeler in Macon for ba-
sic training.

Livingston studied the men as they approached.
Colon's swarthy looks and swagger reminded him
of the street corner hoods who used to tease him
back in New York, calling him Bookworm and
Clay Ton. That is, until he hit the puberty speed-
way, slimming down and shooting up to six-feet-
two. And learned judo. And knocked the two front
teeth from the mouth of Vinnie Papa when he
pulled a switchblade.

Ernesto Colon. A punk. Kenneth Ogan. A soft-
spoken noncom with no combat experience running the show.

Christ.

Not a promising start for what Ogan had de-
scribed as "the most important mission of the
war."

The new arrivals climbed the staircase.

"Good morning, Sergeant," Ogan said to Livingston. "It's good to see you again." He introduced Colon. "Sergeant Livingston, this is—"

"I know. Ernesto Colon. Nice to meet you, soldier."

Ogan was taken aback. "You know? How?"

"Maher told me."

"He *what*?" Ogan looked shocked.

Livingston's brow wrinkled. "Told me. I don't follow—is that a problem?"

"A problem?" Outwardly, Ogan remained calm, but his voice was agitated. "Don't you people believe in *security*? Don't you realize we're at *war*!"

"Yes, Sergeant Major. But with the Germans, not with each other."

"And who are *you* to say where spies might be hiding? Good God, there are *reasons* for caution!"

Before Livingston could reply, the Englishman turned and made his way to the cockpit.

Colon put down his gear. "I hate to say it, Sergeant, but we've got ourselves a real by-the-book *somaro*."

Livingston looked over. "Excuse me?"

"A jackass, Sergeant. A bunghole."

Livingston scowled. "That may be, Private, but he's still running the show."

Colon's eyes grew hooded. "Yes, Sergeant," he said, his voice barely audible.

Colon shouldered past, Livingston convinced that he'd made a point of brushing against his chest as he did so. The sergeant clenched his fists. It was going to be a long flight. He only hoped that the rest of the war—not to mention the rest of the team—was an improvement. . . .

Chapter Two

Corporal Arthur "Wings" Weyers had done other dangerous things in his life.

Two years before, he'd stolen a Gladiator biplane and crashed it while chasing a Nazi aircraft outside of Pretoria. A year later, he'd impersonated a dead officer in order to get into Britain's Hurricane squadron. Both times he was brought up on charges and then pardoned. Both times his commanding officers recognized that the objective had justified the extraordinary means.

But this . . .

This was insane. Yet Lambert *was* a fellow soldier and, dangerous as this mission was, loyalty mattered above all. Even though he'd only just met Lambert the day before.

Jean-Pierre Lambert. The Rotter . . . or whatever it was he called himself in French. He'd said it stood for stealth. Uncanny senses. Agility. The gift of gab.

Still, the giant South African wished that Lambert hadn't practiced the gift on *him*. He'd been able to explain the crashed Gladiator, the stolen dogtags. But how would he justify this?

Well, Inspector Sweet, sir, Corporal Lambert here felt it would be a jolly good test of our skills if we snuck out of our own hotel room while you gentlemen waited for the two men from America.

The grunts from behind were distracting. Weyers looked around the nearly empty cinema, then tried to concentrate on the movie.

Without success.

There wasn't even a good-looking woman on the screen. Just a bald-headed scientist named Dr. Cyclops, who'd shrunk a group of people to the size of dolls. Right now the little people were busy trying to load a giant shotgun and shoot the sleeping scientist.

Behind him, Audrey started to moan. Weyers shook his head. Where had he gone wrong? He and Lambert had both been to the same pub the night before. They'd both made a good impression. They'd both laughed when she pointed out her husband, a monstrously obese man who had passed out in a booth across the room. And there was no question which of the two men had the better build.

But it was Lambert, the runt, that Audrey asked to see the next day.

Weyers sneaked a look back. The young brunette was on her knees, her cheek pressed to the seat cushion; Lambert was behind her, bent over, his chin in her shoulder.

Weyers sighed weakly—then gasped as he looked down the aisle and saw a corpulent silhouette moving toward the writhing couple. The newcomer was holding something, a newspaper. He turned into their row, and Weyers was instantly on his feet.

The shotgun blast on the screen erupted at the same instant that Weyers's fist snapped the nose of the startled fat man. Blood spilled over the newcomer's rolling chins and bowtie. Lambert looked up.

"*Qu'est-ce que*—"

In response, Weyers reached over the seat and yanked his disoriented comrade up by the shirt collar. Lambert stumbled over his trousers as they rushed down the aisle.

"Wings, what—"

"Not *now*!"

The woman was still screaming, but from shock rather than passion. Lambert stopped and looked back, but Weyers pulled him along by the arm. They made their way out a fire exit into a bright alley. Weyers pushed the smaller man ahead, then hurried back and put an ear to the door. Lambert did up his pants.

"Damn it, Wings, what the hell did you *do* back there?"

"Saved you." Weyers listened. There were muffled shouts inside, but no one was coming. He returned to his friend. "I don't know which of us is the bigger idiot!"

"Why?"

" 'Cheaper than a hotel,' you said. 'No one will be here in the middle of the day.' "

"What are you talking about? I was *right*!"

"Oh, you were right. No one was there—*except the lady's bloody husband!*"

Lambert's jaw fell. "*Zut!* Is *that* who that was?"

"The same, and he was holding a newspaper. She must have been looking at the movie adverts back at the house, left it open."

Lambert whistled. "Such a nice bosom . . . but so stupid!"

"Who, you or her? Or maybe *me*! That could

have been nasty, Rotter. Public lewdness, an arrest, Sweet or Escott having to bail us out—"

The men walked in silence toward the street. They poked their heads around the corner, glanced toward the front of the movie theater; when no one came out, they walked quickly in the other direction.

Lambert had told him not to worry about what they were doing. If there was anything seven years of soldiering had taught him, it was *never* to worry about the future. In all likelihood, they wouldn't be around to suffer it.

But Weyers was a worrier, and always would be. And right now, the South African was glad about that.

"I owe you one," Lambert said at last. "Even though the lady finished and I didn't—I owe you."

"Just get us back into our room," Weyers said glumly, "and we'll be square."

Lambert's smile indicated he had no doubt they'd get back inside. Somehow. It might not be as clean or easy as the way they'd gotten out, going through the window of Lambert's seventh-floor room and leaping down to the roof of an adjoining apartment house. As Weyers had astutely pointed out when they made their way down that building's stairwell, leaping back *up* a story wouldn't be easy.

But Lambert would find a way. He always found a way.

Since his childhood in Sousse, Tunisia, where his father served with the French Foreign Legion, Jean-Pierre Lambert had been called *Le Rôdeur*— the Prowler. The name stemmed from an incident in which a diligent search of trash cans at his French lycée had turned up the discarded typewriter ribbon on which an examination paper had been composed. That discovery, and the subsequent deciphering of the questions, had made Lambert a hero to the students at the French school—though a guilt-stricken classmate, a young girl, had eventually revealed his transgression to the teacher, earning him twenty whacks with a ruler and a failing grade.

Lambert had acquired his nickname from the escapade, and he'd also learned two important lessons: never to share information with strangers, and never to put his trust in a woman. Enjoy them, yes, as often as possible, but count on them—never. Audrey's ineptitude merely reinforced his resolve.

The men turned onto Connaught Street in the Bayswater district. As they neared the stately Collins Hotel, Lambert's brown eyes were constantly in motion. He glanced from a bakery to a shoe repair shop to a currency exchange. Suddenly, he slapped Weyers on the chest.

"There!" He pointed triumphantly.

"What?"

"Come with me," Lambert said, and the two men hurried across the busy thoroughfare, Weyers shaking his head all the while.

"Don't worry, *mon ami*. Everything will be fine!"

Lambert's distrust of women ran almost as deep as his innate trust of fellow soldiers. But that was only one of the things that had drawn him to this big man whose bald head and heavily tattooed arms reminded Lambert of someone who might have been a sideshow attraction in the market at Tunis. The night before, when they'd been given a pass, Weyers had proven himself a good listener. He'd paid close attention while Lambert told him and Audrey of his escapades with the Foreign Le-

gion and with de Gaulle's Free French Forces in
London; when pressed, Weyers had openly and
unpretentiously admitted his own triumphs and
misfortunes.

And Weyers had demonstrated his loyalty today. His devotion sent chills down Lambert's
spine.

"So?" Weyers said. "We're here."

"Now." Lambert grinned. "We're going to get
back inside *and* be heroes."

Lambert ducked into the shop and returned a
few minutes later with a sack of chemicals and a
bowtie. Then they hurried to the hotel, Weyers's
ruddy features paling as the Frenchman explained his plan.

Ogan stared out at Hyde Park as the black sedan hurried past.

As he had countless times over the past few
days, he found himself thinking, *If only Barker
were safe.* It would be so much easier with just
himself to worry about. But not knowing whether
his friend was dead or alive, not knowing whether
there'd be an opportunity to save him . . .

He tried to think of something else, of the mission, but as the thick, old trees passed by the window, all he could remember were the times he and
Barker had come here as children. One day in particular stood out. They were fourteen and were
playing spy, eavesdropping on people from behind
trees and benches. For over an hour they'd listened, fascinated, to a wounded war veteran telling a friend of the horrors he'd seen in France.
Afterward, seated by the Victoria Gate, both boys
had sworn to do everything they could to spare
others that kind of suffering.

Even if Ogan hadn't agreed with the cause, there

was no reason for him to stay at home. The illegitimate son of a publican, Ogan had been raised by an aunt who spent more time flitting through British society than raising her nephew. He didn't even bother to tell her when he left with Barker to join the army as a boy entrant.

In time, the army sent the youths their separate ways, Ogan to the Army Physical Training School at Aldershot as a sergeant, Barker to the Secret Intelligence Service's Aeronautical Research and Sales Corporation—a facade for photo reconnaissance. There, he not only flew missions over Germany and the Mediterranean, but also he developed a means of using the heating system of the Lockheed 12A to keep the camera lens from frosting over at high altitudes.

Ogan suspected that his fanaticism about his friend, and about punishing those who might have harmed him, was the reason he'd been picked to head this team. That, plus the fact that he was expendable.

They all were. Good men who didn't quite fit anywhere else.

Ogan looked at Livingston and Colon. After just one week with Sweet and Escott, there was no way that they and the other two men would be ready. Before being made a field operative in 1939, Barker had had six weeks at the Royal United Service Institution, a tight but complete course in espionage and survival. These men would be given only the basics at a makeshift facility. The Allied war machine was in motion and they were needed to do a job. Whether they came back was incidental, as long as they helped to undermine the enemy.

The car turned down Edgware Road, just before

the Marble Arch. In the distance, Ogan saw a crowd gathered in the street.

He tapped the driver on the shoulder. "Speed up, would you? There's something going on."

As they neared the hotel, he saw the guests of the Collins clustered in the street; there was a horrible stench in the air, and orange clouds rolled from the upper floors. The driver pulled over and Ogan ran toward the entrance, followed by Livingston and Colon. Sweet and Escott met him outside.

"What the hell happened?"

The chunky Escott was still wiping tears from his eyes. "We were bombed out."

"*What?*"

"Not us . . . not our people. A philandering wife, it appears." The balding man held up a broken bottle. "Sulphur dioxide. Hit a row of rooms along the back. Also the kitchen and the ballroom."

"Any idea who or why?"

Escott gestured toward Lambert, who was sitting on a fire hydrant. Weyers was standing beside him, his arms folded tightly across his chest.

"They both heard a crash and went to the window. Said they saw a man on the roof next door and chased him."

"They *jumped* down?"

"About twelve feet. Weyers actually cracked the tile."

"And?"

"They got this during a struggle with the chap." Escott pulled a bowtie from his pocket. "They also heard a woman yelling at him from one of the rooms. His name was Derek; hers was Audrey. He was screaming bloody murder about her stinking like the skunk she was."

"A jealous husband tailing his wife," the lanky Sweet interjected.

"We've alerted Scotland Yard," Escott continued. "They'll check marriage records to try to find them. Also, Weyers thinks he broke the man's nose, which should make things a little easier. But I told the chief inspector not to do anything until we're gone, so we don't have to answer questions about what we were doing here."

Ogan filled with pride. "They're good men, Bertie. Damn good men." He glanced at Lambert and nodded at the Frenchman.

Lambert threw a two-fingered salute in return. Weyers just shook his head and groaned quietly.

Chapter Three

Livingston was exhausted. He hadn't slept during the twelve-hour flight. He'd spent most of the time writing letters home, to his father, to his brother . . . and, at long last, to Anna.

Livingston still felt hollow inside when he thought about her. He didn't have many regrets in his life. He mourned the state of the world, which was why he'd left his history studies at NYU and spent two years with the Republicans in Spain, fighting Franco. Even after being captured and sentenced to death, Livingston had been undaunted. Escaping, he'd made his way to France where, still bursting with idealism, he'd fought with the underground until Pearl Harbor. It had been invigorating to him, a chance to *do* something rather than read about what others had done.

Anna never really understood that. When he first mentioned going to Spain, she'd told him to choose between her and his convictions; he'd done the only thing his conscience would allow. But Livingston had never stopped loving her, and he wanted her to know that.

Just in case he never got to tell her in person.

* * *

At the busy London airport, there were more
servicemen coming and going than there were
commercial passengers. A car met Livingston, Colon, and Ogan and there was a long delay as trucks
unloaded old eight-inch Howitzers. Livingston
recognized the heavy artillery as being from the
last war, and he guessed that someone, somewhere, must be in desperate shape if these relics
were being trotted out.

He smiled as the old pre-Spain resolve came
flooding back.

The car took them to the Collins Hotel. There,
they were shown to a suite. While Ogan, Sweet,
and Escott reviewed maps before the briefing, the
rest of the men sat in a corner of the room, smoking cigarettes and sipping beer. Ogan had told
them to get to know one another, and it didn't take
long for Livingston to peg Lambert and Weyers,
his other two new colleagues.

He listened politely while Lambert recounted
the story of the jealous husband and his stink
bombs.

"How do you think he got onto the roof?" the
American asked when the Frenchman was finished.

"Up the stairwell, I'd imagine. Let me assure
you from experience, Sergeant, an enraged husband knows no obstacles."

The bowtie was sitting on an end table. Livingston leaned over and sniffed it. He frowned. "I
don't think so."

"Eh?"

"I don't think he climbed the stairwell."

"No?"

Livingston shook his head. "A man as fat as you

say would have perspired, walking up six flights in the summer heat. That tie doesn't smell bad. For that matter, it doesn't even smell as though it's been *worn*."

Lambert smiled sickly, and Weyers's expression grew dark.

The American leaned closer. "In fact, I don't think the husband was even here."

Lambert's thin lips tightened ominously. "What do you mean?"

"I smell perfume."

"So? Whoever had this room before—"

"I smell perfume on *you*, Lambert, and I smell a rat in your story." Livingston sat back. He took a sip of beer, the angry eyes of the Frenchman still upon him. "You want me to spell it out? You two were supposed to be in the hotel resting, just like Private Colon and I were supposed to do on the plane. But you went AWOL, and made up this cockamamy story to cover it."

Weyers sat stone-still. Lambert arched a thin brow.

"Tell me," said the Frenchman, "were you a detective in the States?"

"No. I just have a habit of watching people, and thinking about what I see."

"Thinking, maybe a bit *too* much."

Livingston snickered. "It's been suggested before."

"Suppose I tell you you're right," Lambert went on. "What would you do?"

Livingston shrugged. "Nothing. As long as you don't lam when I'm counting on you, I don't give a goddamn how you spend your free time."

Weyers looked behind him, then pulled his chair forward. "May I speak freely, Sergeant?" Livingston nodded and the big South African cocked his

thumb toward the Frenchman. "Let me tell you a
little something about Lambert here. When he was
eleven, his father and an entire Legion patrol disappeared in the southern desert. Do you know
what the boy did? Ran away from home and survived a year in that region until he found his dad's
grave . . . and also rescued two Legionnaires who'd
been taken to Arab prisons. He's a *survivor*, so am
I—and those who are with us survive as well." He
grew agitated now. "I've broken rules and I've
lied, but I've never abandoned a comrade. Now I
ask you—can I count on *you* to do the same? To
throw yourself on a potato masher if the need
arises?"

Livingston sat back. "I've done it, pal, many
times."

Weyers's eyes went wide.

"As a matter of fact," Livingston deadpanned,
"I swallowed one at Châlons-sur-Marne. Managed
to spit it back at the Heinies, though, just before
it went off."

Lambert grinned. "You have a sense of humor."
He offered Livingston his hand. "That's good. I
know I can count on a man who doesn't take life
so seriously." He turned and glanced at Colon,
who was sitting quietly off to one side, nursing a
beer and reading a *Captain America* comic book.
"And what about you, Private? Would you fall on
a grenade for your comrades?"

"I ain't that stupid," Colon said without looking
up.

Lambert frowned. "No? Perhaps, then, you're in
the wrong business, monsieur."

Colon's expression didn't change. "Perhaps,
missyure, you're just a bad businessman. I believe
in shootin' someone *before* he can lob a grenade
at me."

The Frenchman's expression brightened. "Touché." He extended his hand again. Colon shook it. "I believe we all understand each other now, *n'est-ce pas?*"

Livingston and Weyers raised their glasses and toasted Lambert's declaration; Colon sat back and regarded Ogan and his two aides.

"Sure," he said, "we'll get along. The question is—doin' what?"

Ogan rolled a blackboard from the corner. He wrote a name on it, then stood to one side.

"Thank you for your patience, gentlemen. Unfortunately, we're all doing a bit of catching up here, as the need for the operation took us all by surprise."

Ogan pointed to the name.

"Harold Barker," he said softly, "is a good friend of mine. A good friend, and a damn fine intelligence agent. His work for the Secret Intelligence Service is legendary. Three years ago, he snuck into Freidrichshafen, to investigate rumors that Hitler was about to recommission the *Graf Zeppelin* for bombing raids over England. Shortly after that, he parachuted into Augsburg to report on the tests of the fast new Messerschmitt fighters, with which the RAF has since become quite familiar. His last mission, recently completed, was a trip to a Hamburg plant to take a look at a new German warplane, the Focke-Wulf 190. I tell you this so you'll understand that he is not a man who slips up. Yet last week, while on a reconnaissance mission to Algiers, Barker was captured. Gentlemen, *we* are going to Algiers, and though a seasoned professional failed, we must not."

The men seemed unfazed. Ogan was encouraged.

"Very soon, the Americans will be taking part in their first military action of the war, an invasion of the northern coast of Africa. We are going to pave the way for that invasion. Obviously, Barker's capture is disastrous for two reasons. First, our team was to use the information he was sent to acquire. Second, the SIS didn't receive a single transmission after Barker was put ashore. This suggests that the Germans knew he was coming, which means there may be a leak somewhere in the network, either at the SIS itself or abroad." He looked at Livingston. "That's why I was rather agitated at the airfield when I learned of your superior's indiscretion. There are already too many loose lips, too many open ears."

Livingston nodded with understanding.

"The leak is the reason that Military Intelligence, and not the SIS, brought in Inspectors Sweet and Escott from Scotland Yard. Both men have considerable experience in the areas that will be needed to turn us into a successful fighting *unit*"—he paused and looked at each man—"a unit whose job is *vital*. One week from tomorrow, we will be taken to North Africa by submarine. Our task is to disrupt activity at an aerodrome located south of Algiers. We must succeed not just because of the tactical stakes for the Allies, but because the only way *we'll* be getting out is after the Allied forces have made a successful landing."

"The proverbial do or die," Lambert said.

"In a nutshell, yes. Are there any questions so far?"

Lambert lit a cigarette. "Blowing up an airfield . . . that takes a lot of firepower. Why not just send in bombers?"

"For a number of reasons. Antiaircraft fire would be prohibitively thick, especially at the low altitudes we'd have to fly to make accurate strikes. Nor can we be sure of the weather there, and delays would be catastrophic. Finally, the strikes must be unexpected. We mustn't leave the Germans time to bring in additional aircraft or troops to repel the Allied invasion."

"And the explosives?" Livingston asked. "We can't just sneak in that kind of artillery on our backs."

"Sufficient weapons and TNT will be there for us, at a farm outside Algiers."

Livingston's expression soured. "I thought your sources in the region may have been compromised. How can you count on them for matériel?"

"There *is* a risk," Ogan admitted, "but we believe it's an acceptable one."

"Acceptable—to whom?"

"To the generals and to *me*. I'm satisfied that the two people we've involved can be trusted. Both have proven themselves repeatedly. Delphine Dupre has been with the Resistance since 1940, and a chicken farmer, Chadli Abdelghani, detests the Nazis for having killed his wife and sons."

"A chicken farmer," Lambert muttered. "What will we do, lob explosive eggs?"

"I'll hear none of *that*," Ogan snapped. "Mr. Abdelghani would not hesitate to lay down his life for the mission—or for any one of you."

"I assume he'll also be our guide?" Livingston said.

Ogan shook his head. "He's wanted by the Nazis, and will have to lay low. But Lambert spent time with the Foreign Legion in Algiers, and with what he knows of the region, and with briefings, we should be able to get through this just fine." He paused, rubbed his hands slowly. His anger had passed. "I know that all of you were ordered to volunteer for this assignment. However, I believe that no team can function well unless all of its members are committed. If any of you cares to resign at this time, I'll find a way for him to do so."

Weyers shook his head at once. Everyone but Livingston sat stone-still.

The American squirmed in his seat.

"Is there a problem?" Ogan asked.

"I'm not sure."

"What does *that* mean?"

"I'm not afraid to go in there," Livingston said, "despite the doubts I have about relying on partisans who have Krauts watching every piss they take. But I get the feeling *you're* not telling us everything."

Now it was Ogan who shifted uncomfortably. "I beg your pardon?"

"It's just a feeling. You seem distracted."

"I am. By the mission."

"I don't mean that. Maybe distracted's a bad word. You seem preoccupied."

After a long, tense silence, Ogan said, "I assure you, I'm as full of the mission as any man here. However, if my manner is going to affect your performance in any way, let me know now."

Livingston glanced at Sweet and Escott, who seemed even more surprised than Ogan by the charge. He slumped in his seat. "No. Not at all. And if I'm wrong, I apologize."

Ogan said that he understood. But his face was pale, and Livingston's expression suggested that his own fears hadn't been allayed.

Ogan thanked the men and explained that in the morning, they would be driven to a special facility in an abandoned warehouse on the Thames. There, Escott and Sweet would refine their talents further, turning these men of diverse backgrounds and natures into the single-minded unit code-named Force Five.

Hearing that Escott and Sweet were going to be the ones to train them, Lambert and Weyers exchanged dubious glances. But as they and the others were to discover, the pair's quiet, outwardly kind demeanor was as deceptive as the appearance of the warehouse itself.

Livingston hung up the telephone. It was 0300; Ogan had just told him to be downstairs in half an hour. Though the group had been informed that they'd be awakened earlier each day, getting onto a schedule that had more waking hours at night than during the day didn't make *doing* it any easier.

The sergeant did one hundred push-ups to get his blood flowing, then dragged himself into the closet-size bathroom. There, as usual, his mind quickly shifted into gear. The doubts of the previous evening had diminished; sleep, along with the anticipation of getting to work, was invigorating. He was wide awake by the time he got downstairs.

Ogan, Colon, and Weyers looked no different— no more pleasant, no less dour—than they had the day before, although Lambert looked as if he hadn't slept. Most likely he hadn't; a maid winked at him when she came downstairs. The Frenchman dozed during the twenty-five-minute drive to the Castorp Trading Company on the Cadogan Pier.

The automobile headlights were turned off several blocks from their destination, and the driver proceeded slowly—not, Ogan pointed out, for concern about any stray pedestrians, but rather, to keep their approach as silent as possible.

"Your humanity is touching," Lambert mumbled, his eyes still shut.

When the car stopped, the men were ushered quickly into the building.

From the brief glimpse he'd gotten of the exterior, Livingston could see that few changes had been made to turn the small warehouse into a training facility. It had been selected, Livingston learned, for several reasons. For one, the building was just the right size and shape to suit the team's needs: large enough to accommodate the necessary equipment, but small enough to create a sense of intimacy, of five people functioning as a team. For another, this region of the Thames had been badly damaged during the Luftwaffe's bombing raids two years before. A passerby would have suspected nothing out of the ordinary if he saw workers coming and going, boarding up the windows and doors—so snugly that not a trace of light leaked from inside—carrying in crates and cartons that contained everything from pistol targets to sheets of sound-absorbing material for the walls. What's more, because businesses had abandoned the area, anyone who came poking around would be easily seen and could be watched from the rooftops of adjoining buildings. This surveillance was constant; anyone who approached would be spotted and photographed. The hope was that if enemy agents managed to learn of the preparations and tried to find out the men's identities, they would be apprehended.

Sweet and Escott were already inside. Both men were dressed in black trousers and T-shirts, and they handed the others identical outfits. The two trainers had obviously come here directly from the hotel meeting because the warehouse was warm; a compact electrical heater in each corner churned out waves of heat. Livingston later learned that everything in the facility was run by electricity, so that no smoke or other signs of habitation would be visible from the outside.

When everyone was dressed, the tall, spindly Sweet had them line up. He paced before them.

"The schedule here will be a simple one," he said in his high, nasal voice. "Limbering exercises first off, then instruction in physical combat. I know you gentlemen have had experience in this, but we will refine your skills. In the case of some of you, such as Sergeant Livingston, who is proficient in the martial arts, you will be asked to work with the others. You see, when you joined the military, most of you were instructed to capture rather than kill your adversaries. That will no longer apply.

"A meal break will be followed by your weapons class. Again, Sergeant Major Ogan is exceptionally proficient with handguns, and Corporal Lambert with a dagger. They will be called upon to help the others."

The bookish Escott then came forward to explain the subjects of the lectures that he would give in the afternoons: the topography of the area where they were going, the kinds of aircraft they would need to recognize, training in the handling and deployment of all kinds of explosives, and finally, conversational German. In the last, Livingston and Ogan had distinct advantages. Both spoke the language fluently, Livingston having grown up on New York's Upper East Side, with its large German population, and Ogan having studied the language at Aldershot. The others knew just enough to get by. Lambert remarked that he was looking forward to these lessons because the only words he'd used in years were *fraulein* and *shtupp*.

For his levity, Lambert was called upon to help Sweet get the classes under way: as a model for demonstrating the various ways of breaking a man's neck.

The lecture that Livingston found at once most important and most lacking was the one involving the German air base itself. The only reference material was aerial reconnaissance photos taken more than a month before—and not photographs of the aerodrome per se but of the beaches. Because of frequent patrols coming and going from the field, as well as batteries of antiaircraft guns to forestall Allied bombing raids, material on the aerodrome was scarce and incomplete. The best picture they had was a mosaic showing some eighty percent of the field. The men were told that was all they needed to see because it showed the northern, beachward approach that they would be taking.

The group would be required to move southeast, crossing a ten-kilometer stretch of alternately mountainous and sparsely wooded countryside dominated by the towering, 1,830-meter-high peak Djebel Ouarsenis. On the other side was the airfield. Because the Germans used the roads to go around the mountain, only peasants would see them as they crossed the low-lying foothills in their German uniforms. No one would ask why they were traveling alone or where they were going. If everything went well, they could hide outside the gate and then use their documents to go through with a group of returning soldiers.

"If for some reason security is breached," Escott said, "and you have to be less visible, there are no fences; just four watchtowers, one at each of the field's corners. You can hide beneath any of the clusters of trees near the field, wait until nightfall, then sneak in."

That sounded too easy, and Livingston said so; but Escott dismissed his fears with a wave of his hand.

"The Germans don't expect an attack by land, and certainly not by a small band of commandos. Intelligence reports indicate—and the photographs bear this out—that they anticipate an air raid to precede any invasion. It's the small crack in their dike which will allow the floodwaters to enter."

Livingston still wasn't convinced, but no one was about to alter any plans for him. It was apparent that he and his teammates were expendable, more so than the hundred or so aircraft they might lose in a bombing raid.

Sweet and Escott proved to be able coaches. Although neither had had any espionage experience since the last war, neither had any ties to the intelligence community. Thus, whoever was leaking information at the SIS would have no knowledge about the instructors, their men, or the mission.

The government pair was also tireless. At night, when the men would curl up on the cots that had been arranged in the corner of the warehouse, the two inspectors huddled under a lamp and continued to study their maps and dossiers. The next day, any new information that might prove useful was added to the lessons.

That included any facts they learned about the men. In Livingston's case, they found out about the nicknames he'd hated as a child. During knife practice with Weyers, the American was pinned and about to have the tip of a rubber blade thrust under his jaw. Sweet chose that moment to refer

to him as Bookworm, and Livingston grew livid.
Weyers never knew what hit him. Livingston literally lifted him off the ground and flipped him
over. The American was advised to remember the
hatred that name elicited, and to draw upon it
when necessary. For his part, Weyers was told to
remember how mortified *he* was getting up after
the match.

The instructors also found something that
moved Ogan, although not in the way that they'd
expected. They told him, during target practice,
that he was shooting at the Gestapo officer who
had captured Barker. Ogan stopped firing, lowered the pistol, and stood still for a long moment.

Escott went over to him. "What's wrong?"

"Nothing." Ogan quietly resumed firing and
missed not only the sheets of paper that had been
tacked to the sandbags, but also the sandbags
themselves. The bullets ricocheted off the corru-
gated metal of the wall behind the targets, sending the team scurrying for safety. Ogan didn't
move: He just continued firing until the gun was
empty. When he began to reload, Escott jogged
over and relieved him of the weapon.

Ogan recovered and apologized, but that night
there was quiet discussion between the two instructors and Ogan about what had happened.
Livingston listened intently to the conversation.

"What was going through your mind?" Escott
asked after they'd all poured themselves tea.

Ogan looked down at his cup. "The mission."

"What about it? Not the danger."

"No. About how I have to *finish* what Barker
started. I've never felt a responsibility like that,
and it overwhelmed me."

The men were silent for a minute. "I do hope
you'll forgive me," Escott said, "but I have to ask:

How can we be certain that you won't be overwhelmed again? In Algiers, for example, where it would be disastrous."

"You know me, Bertie. I've never buckled under pressure."

Escott tapped Ogan's dossier. "But you've never had *this* kind of pressure. My god, give credit to Livingston; he saw it in your face the other day."

"Saw what?"

"Preoccupation. We missed it. What's more, we thought your close ties to Barker would encourage you, compensate for your lack of frontline experience. If it turns out that they're *inhibiting* you—"

"I've been close to a *lot* of men who have died. I tell you, what happened today was a fluke." Ogan looked across the room. He saw Livingston staring at him in the dark and turned away. "It won't happen again."

The men fell silent. Sweet sipped his tea. "Frankly, Bertie, I'm inclined to forget this matter. Forewarned is forearmed, and all of that."

Escott lay a hand on Ogan's shoulder. "As you said to the men at orientation, there's no shame in withdrawing from this mission. If you're at all uncertain—"

"I tell you I'm *fine*. I've resigned myself to the fact that Barker is dead, and I've also resigned myself to the fact that I'm the only one who can give his death meaning. I'm not about to leave him with a legacy of failure."

Escott smiled. "I understand, and we're sure you'll come around."

"You have to." Sweet chuckled. "Do you think we'd trust anyone but an Englishman to run this operation?"

"Quite so," Escott added. "I suggest we just forget this matter and see that it doesn't happen again.''

Ogan thanked them, then excused himself and went to the stall shower that occupied most of the bathroom.

Lying with his back to the group, Livingston swore silently. With Ogan and Colon in their own worlds, and Lambert and Weyers opening up mostly to one another, he had never felt more apprehensive about a mission . . . or more vulnerable.

Chapter Four

The week passed quickly.

By the third day, the men were awake at 0130. After five hours of sleep they were learning to roll newspapers into tight, conical knives. Shooting countless targets while trying to ignore the grating of the cement trucks that came by every day, at the same time—ostensibly to do repairs on the dock, but actually to cover the sound of the pistol reports. Throwing the other team members and being thrown. Memorizing names of streets in Algiers, studying the height and location of hills, plains, mountains, and streams. Lambert was even called upon to do some last-minute tailoring when Weyers dropped five pounds during the week and his German uniform had to be taken in.

It was also drilled into the men that if anything happened to any team member, if they were wounded or captured, the mission was still to come first. A wounded man could be left with their Algerian contact at his chicken farm; a captured man was the property of the Nazis until the invasion was completed. The latter sat easily with everyone but Colon, who asked if it didn't make

more sense to try and rescue someone rather than
go to the airfield with too few men.

"If just one man gets through to the aerodrome," Escott had said, "he can destroy at least
one aircraft. That will save countless lives. The
mission," he stressed, "must come first."

That, Livingston realized, was really the reason they had all been brought to the warehouse.
The skills everyone had learned might prove valuable, but the new knowledge wasn't as important as utter immersion in their goal. The
warehouse was a place where the world had been
shut out, where a neutral environment had been
created. There was only the mission. The aerodrome. The notion that a plane for a life was a
fair exchange. The unspoken rule was to work
closely with the team members, but not to *get*
close to them.

When they finally left the facility in the small
hours of the morning of November 3, 1942, each
man was preoccupied with the job at hand. The
war was something other people were handling.
For them, until the invasion force landed in five
days, there was only Algiers.

As they drove to the submarine base at South-
ampton, Sweet reviewed the schedule. Their *Saphir* submarine would put them ashore near
Algiers at approximately 2200 hours on November
5, after which they would head for the city and a
kiosk run by Delphine Dupre. Ogan was to approach and ask for a copy of *Doc Savage* magazine. The woman would then give him directions
to the farmhouse that Resistance forces had used
until they were slain following an attack against
German officers headed for a visit with the sultan
of Morocco.

Still dressed in black, each man carried the uniform of a German mechanic, which they would don before arriving; each man had also been equipped with a Walther P.38 service pistol.

Sweet reviewed the jobs each man was to undertake. When they entered the aerodrome, Ogan, Weyers, and Colon were to reconnoiter. Lambert and Livingston were charged with hiding and detonating the explosives. In the event that team members were captured or killed, the reconnaisance was to be scrapped.

"Just go in and *hit* them," Escott said. "Use common sense."

"But that *won't* be necessary," Sweet averred. "As Bertie and I have told you repeatedly, if you do your job, no one will *know* you are the enemy."

Like Barker, Livingston thought as they made their way through the dark British countryside. The more he thought about what Sweet said, the more it sounded like famous last words— particularly with Ogan in charge.

Although the Englishman had overcome his initial panic and proved himself to be an exceptional marksman, Livingston noticed that he still had a tendency to analyze too much. Intellectuals made great tacticians but lousy leaders.

No matter. Though the spirit of freedom and adventure that had infected him in Spain was not present here, it could be worse: He could be back shuffling papers behind a desk. Unlike Ogan, Livingston welcomed the opportunity to focus on the mission instead of on the past.

As Captain Geoffrey Thorpe was quick to point out, the *Saphir* was seaworthy, but just barely.

Neither the submarine nor its crew had rested in weeks, and the strain showed on both.

A French minelayer, the *Saphir* had been scuttled at Toulon in 1940; reclaimed by the British, it was put into service as a decoy in the Mediterranean, chasing enemy ships toward the more valuable U-class submarines that preyed on Axis convoys. Although one of the more modern vessels was at the disposal of the SIS, and had been used to ferry Barker to Algiers, Escott had gone right to the Admiralty's Intelligence Section for this ship. Even Thorpe didn't know their destination until Ogan provided it.

When informed, the burly, red-bearded Welshman glowered at the group gathered on the dark, windswept dock.

"Some cargo. Y'look like a minstrel show. And some journey. Seventeen hundred nautical miles here, seventeen hundred back, all of it through some of the Naziest waters on God's blue earth. Not what we were hoping for when we were recalled."

"My apologies," Ogan said curtly. "We've all been working long hours."

"Not cooped up in a leaking tub o' foul air, y'haven't."

Sweet stepped between them. "I'm afraid *everyone's* going to have to make the best of this, Captain. Furthermore, as you've no doubt been informed—but I'll remind you anyway, since you're so sorely overworked—you are to refrain from any and all radio communication during the mission. Your location is not to be revealed for *any* reason. Is that clear?"

Thorpe spit in the river. "Clear as a parson's eyes."

"That includes any SOS you might receive."

"I *said* your orders were clear."

Colon came forward and faced Ogan. "May I go aboard, Sergeant? I already decked my quota of officers for the month."

Ogan regarded Thorpe, whose blue eyes shrunk to slits. "Are ye threatening me, little man?"

"He was talking to me—" Ogan said.

"But meanin' me. Are ye *threatening* me, Private?"

Colon set his gear on the dock. As he turned to face Thorpe, Livingston walked over and grabbed his arms. "Don't, Private. *Save* it. Let it out later."

"There'll be plenty left over—"

"Not if you get shipped home. We *need* you."

"With crow in my yap?"

"I've eaten nestfuls. It goes down hard, but it goes down. This just isn't worth jeopardizing the mission."

The private pursed and unpursed his lips, then said in a barely audible voice, "No, Captain, sir. I was not threatening you."

The captain's chest inflated and his expression was self-righteous. "Very well. Permission to go aboard granted. But mind me, Private. Talk like that again and ye'll ride to North Africa in a bleedin' torpedo tube."

His dark eyes hard, Colon elbowed stiffly past the Captain and went to the conning tower. Livingston regarded Thorpe. "When we get back, Captain, I'll want to see you myself. Your attitude needs some improving."

"Ye're welcomed to try me, hero."

"*Moi aussi!*" Lambert said, rattling a fist. "I may not be able to reach your fuzzy chin, but I can wreak considerable damage on your fuzzy elsewheres!"

"I'll handle the chin," Weyers promised. "In fact, why don't we make it us five against your whole stinking crew? We can use the exercise!"

"All right," Sweet cut in, "enough of this." He shooed Lambert and Weyers ahead. But there was a sparkle in his eye and he held Ogan back; after the captain had gone aboard, Escott came over from the car.

"Quite unexpected, but did you *see*?" Sweet asked.

Escott nodded.

Ogan was confused. "See what?"

"Tell me you didn't notice!" Sweet said with a cheek-splitting smile. "Your men. They just worked as a *team*. When we drove over, Livingston wasn't talking to Colon, nor Lambert to Livingston. But just now, they backed each other up. It was magnificent!"

"Kennie, don't let them get into any scraps on board," Escott cautioned, "but don't discourage grumbling and moaning as long as it's just between them. The closer they feel, the better they'll function in Algiers."

Ogan nodded, then headed for the ship.

"And, Kennie—one thing more."

Ogan looked back.

"Good luck. When you come back, dinner is on me."

Thanking him, Ogan climbed the ladder and disappeared into the tower.

The two-day journey was marked by tedium and a strained truce between crew and passengers. Because of the cramped quarters, when they weren't sleeping, the five passengers had to sit huddled together in the small, dark corner of the torpedo deck. It also happened to be the loudest part of the ship, which, they were convinced, was why Thorpe had put them there.

They sat on the floor, their knees to their chins, as men moved by. Sometimes they stood so the blood could circulate in their legs. Quite often they cursed so that they wouldn't be angry enough to grab Thorpe whenever he'd walk by.

They passed the time by recounting what they'd done in the past, what they needed to remember about the near future, and what they hoped to do in the distant future.

At one point, Livingston asked Ogan about Harold Barker. He watched the Englishman closely: Ogan didn't disappoint him. He talked a little about the past, about how much he loved and admired the man. And all the while he had the same look in his eyes that he'd had in London.

Livingston wanted to believe that it was just grief that was affecting his teammate. But Ogan had the look of a man with a personal agenda, and Livingston resolved to watch him as closely as he did the Germans.

It was nearly 2330 when the submarine reached the coast of Algeria. The five men knew it because it suddenly became much quieter in their dark corner.

Ogan checked his watch. "Not bad. Only ninety-odd minutes late."

"Assuming that bastard Thorpe hasn't sailed to Germany to put us ashore," Weyers noted.

"Let him!" Lambert growled. "The war will be over that much sooner. We'll find Hitler and wring his neck!"

They walked to the bridge, Lambert muttering about what else he'd do to Hitler if he ever encountered the Nazi leader.

When they arrived, Thorpe was at the periscope and his men were already breaking out their gear and the inflatable raft. The captain gave the order to surface.

"Thank you for the uneventful passage," Ogan said formally. "I'm sorry for any distress we caused you."

Thorpe pulled at his beard. "I'll give ye this: Ye've been decent passengers. In spite of yer smart-mouthing men, I wish ye well."

The rush of water echoed through the bridge as the submarine broke the surface. The raft was already in the conning tower, and was quickly pushed through the hatch. The men scurried out after it, Ogan waiting behind to collect the paddles and duffel bags. He passed these to Weyers, who placed them in the raft. Colon and Lambert steadied the boat while Livingston stowed the gear.

The submarine was just over a half mile from shore, and Captain Thorpe waited until the men had covered half that distance before submerging. Even at a quarter mile away, the suction from the vessel tugged hard on the rubber raft.

When the submarine was gone, the only noises the men heard were the slapping of the water against the boat and the gentle sounds of the two paddles.

Colon watched the shoreline closely as they approached. That was Ogan's job; the sergeant major was the one peering through the Swiss binoculars. But Colon watched too from under the long peak of the lightweight field cap he wore. As much as he hated to admit it, sometimes the refs and coaches saw things from the sidelines that the players didn't.

And sometimes, the people were just no good. Even well-meaning people like Ogan.

He remembered vividly the day he walked home from the schoolyard and decided to stop to meet his father as he left the steel mill.

The day. The black day the stock market lost its shirt.

He was twelve, and he remembered the utter silence with which all the workers filed past the gate. He heard the foreman talking to his father and a few of the other men.

"Trust me," he said. "I'll hire you back as soon as things get squared away. It shouldn't be more than a few weeks at the most."

Trust me. Colon could still see the man's fleshy face, still hear the utter sincerity in his voice. Maybe he meant what he said. Maybe he, too, was well meaning. But weeks became months, and his father didn't work again until 1932, when military contracts started coming in. If it hadn't been for his mother's garden, they would have had to steal to survive. As it was, Colon jimmied so many gumball machines in Pittsburgh that a special police detail was put on the case. They watched the machines and he watched them. At night, he would sneak in while they went for coffee. Or took a leak. Or turned to look at a leggy woman. He learned to be quiet, quick, and observant.

And alone.

This team was a good one, just like the team at Duquesne and the team at the base. Sharp, ambitious men. But he still functioned best as a thief in the night, and as he paddled he watched, looking for glints where a gun might reflect light, listening for voices in the dark.

Like Colon, Livingston watched as he paddled.

The beach was surprisingly nondescript, not quite what he'd expected from this exotic land: a narrow stretch of sand with the silhouette of grassy dunes rising gently behind it. Beyond those, to the north, he could just barely make out the black outline of the ancient city and the surrounding hills. It was a clear but moonless night; in the distance the stars suddenly disappeared, blotted out by the jagged Atlas Mountains.

Weyers stared ahead as well, but he was more concerned with keeping the gear from sliding around as they crossed the choppy Mediterranean. Lambert looked toward the shore while he worked the flap of his belt holster, softening it up so it would bend more readily, making the contents more accessible. When he was finished, he did the same with the flaps of his three ammunition pouches.

No one spoke. The shore was less than one hundred meters away.

Suddenly, Colon tapped Ogan on the shoulder. He pointed to a cove just south of where they were headed. Ogan turned the glasses in that direction. Nodding, he handed the binoculars to Lambert. The Frenchman looked out, saw two people embracing on a blanket. Chances were good that the lovers wouldn't hear an LST if it came ashore and started disgorging Sherman tanks.

But chances were something they couldn't take. Returning the binoculars to Ogan, Lambert removed his cap, shoes, and blue green service tunic, then slipped over the side.

Lambert had forgotten how cold fall nights could be in North Africa. He was reminded of his first night in the Legion, when he was stationed some four hundred kilometers to the west, in

Sidi-bel-Abbes. Standing guard over a shipment of rifles, he'd actually paid a week's wages to a boy to fetch him a pot of tea. And it had been worth every sou.

As the chilly waters caused his body temperature to plunge, Lambert had to bite hard to keep his teeth from chattering. For all their smarts, that was something the instructors had forgotten: to waterproof their clothing, or at least have them swim in the Thames to prepare for something like this. On the other hand, he told himself, if he'd known it would be this cold, he might never have volunteered to handle landing security.

At least the current was helping him toward the shore. It would have been unseemly, he felt, if the legendary *Rodeur* had to drag himself ashore, panting.

Less than ten meters from the beach, Lambert stopped and paddled in place. He squinted through the darkness, examining the terrain. He made for the boulders just west of the couple, and when he could stand, he crouched so that just his head was above water. Upon reaching the beach, he dropped to his belly and wriggled toward the rocks. Standing behind the largest of them, he looked over.

They were a young man and woman, either naked or wearing swimsuits, he couldn't tell. Their clothes were piled well away from them; any weapons the man might have brought would be there as well.

Lambert drew his dagger from its metal sheath and crept around the rocks, coming at the couple from behind the man. When there were roughly five meters of beach between him and the lovers, he squatted. Like a cat, he rocked on his haunches before launching forward.

The couple knew that Lambert was there only when he landed on top of them. Lambert buried his blade in the man's throat, while at the same time he kept the woman from screaming by clapping the heel of his hand over her mouth, using the crook of his thumb and index finger to plug her nose. The man clawed at the blade, but only for a moment; gurgling violently, he rolled to his side, blood spurting over the blanket and sand beyond. The woman struggled until Lambert was able to cut her throat.

Lambert rose. With an oath, he examined the spots of blood on his shirt. Recovering his knife, he walked to the sea. He was rubbing at the stains with water when the raft arrived.

Ogan hurried over. "Any trouble?" he whispered.

Lambert shook his head.

"Good work. Colon, Weyers, Livingston ... you take care of the bodies. We'll stow the raft."

The men hauled the boat onto the sands, then hurried over to the blanket. The sight was grotesque; though the man was covered with blood, the woman was the more hideous of the two, her head nearly severed.

"Audrey," Weyers said philosophically as he used the toe of his shoe to cover up the bloody sand. When that was done, he headed behind the rocks and started scooping out a grave while Colon gathered up the bodies. Livingston went through the soldier's clothing, pocketing his identity papers and wallet. When they were finished, they buried the clothes, the blanket, and the deflated raft.

Lambert felt a pang of regret. No doubt this mechanic had sneaked from the aerodrome for a rendezvous with this local girl. The man's motives were probably no different from his own when he'd sneaked from the hotel just a week before, and for the moment at least, the dead man was more like a comrade than an enemy.

When all traces of the couple had been concealed, the men donned the uniforms they'd brought, turned north, and walked along the beach toward the city.

And ran into a carload of Germans coming the other way.

Chapter Five

"They're not supposed to be here," Ogan muttered.

"I thought your Delphine Dupre said that patrols never went farther than a kilometer from the aerodrome," Weyers said.

"That's what she was told," Ogan snapped. "Now be quiet and let me *think*!"

Lambert shook his head as he watched the bullet-shaped Kubel approach. The canvas top was down and he could see five men inside; at least the odds were good.

"They won't be taking us by surprise," he said, repeating the words that Ogan had uttered so confidently. *"Merd!"*

"I said be quiet!"

"They may not even *be* a patrol," Livingston said. "Maybe they're here to pick up their friend."

"I agree," said Ogan, "but in either case, they're going to know we didn't just stroll out here from the airfield."

"I'm not sure about that."

"What do you mean?"

"Maybe we can bluff them."

"How?"

"No time to explain." Livingston started ahead. "Just look like angry sons of bitches and follow my lead."

Ogan frowned. "Weyers, Lambert, stay to the side of the jeep. If anything goes wrong, jump them—knives only."

The group followed a few paces behind Livingston, each man watching intently as the vehicle stopped several meters ahead. The soldier in the passenger side rose and leaned on the windshield. He, like his fellows, were all blackmen—mechanics.

The teenager was wary. "Good evening," he called. "We didn't expect to find anyone else so far from the base."

"Special detail," Livingston answered. "We were sent to find a man who apparently came here without leave." He stepped a bit closer. "May I see *your* papers, please?"

The soldier grinned sheepishly. "We don't have any. We . . . just wanted to see the beach at night."

Ogan and Colon stopped beside Livingston. Weyers and Lambert took up their positions. The Germans regarded them uneasily.

"I wonder," Livingston continued, "could you also have come to pick up this man for whom we are looking? Did you cover for him at the base so he could meet with some *schatze*?"

"*Nein!*" The man laughed. "That would be against regulations!"

Livingston regarded them harshly. He turned to Ogan and whispered. "I think we can take advantage of this. They're afraid. I can order them to take me back to the airfield, maybe pick up intelligence right away."

Ogan scratched his chin. "You mean, separate

into *three* groups? You won't have any backup. Look what happened to Barker—"

"I'm not Barker. I'll watch myself."

Ogan tensed; the remark seemed to decide the matter. "No. I don't want any of my men alone."

"It would only be for tonight. Weyers can still come in tomorrow, as planned, using his papers. He and I will link up somehow. The truth is, I'll be happier if we *do* work separately in there. That way, if one of us screws up—"

"I said no. Escott wanted us to work in teams."

"But Escott didn't know we'd have an opportunity like this. Don't you see it makes more sense than spying by the buddy system?"

"That will be all, Livingston!" Ogan hissed.

The American dug his heels into the sand; Ogan pulled away from him, forcing down his anger as he addressed the Germans.

"We know you're here to find your friend," he called, "but we will take care of that."

"Are you sure? Unless I'm mistaken, there seems to be some problem here."

"Nothing that would concern you. Now go back to the field before we report you as well."

The soldier glanced down at the driver. The invaders couldn't see his expression in the dark.

"Would you like us to take your gear for you? If I may ask, what are you doing with it anyway?"

Ogan stood and stared dumbly at the man. Livingston stepped forward. "No need to hesitate. These men should know what else we're doing, in case they decide to come out here again."

Ogan's eyes were angry. "Then by all means, tell them."

"We've information that advance scouts for the invasion will be landing at this beach. The major felt we should bury mines here, just in case."

The driver rose now and studied the men. "You're not from the explosives unit. Why would the major give you such a detail?"

"We were already coming out to find your friend Engel. We were told to do the other as well, and— foolish us!—we didn't stop to ask the major *why*."

Weyers and Lambert were both studying Livingston in the glare of the headlights. Each man had his hands on his hips, near the hilt of his dagger.

The driver slide from the car. "Mines in duffel bags and a search party instead of police. It all sounds quite strange." He dipped his forehead. "And your shoes are wet. Were you planting your mines in the water?"

The driver reached for his pistol; whirling, Weyers stabbed him in the side, then reached for the man nearest him, pulling him from the backseat onto the sand. Straddling him, Weyers started punching the man in the middle. Lambert, meanwhile, drove his knife into the belly of the man standing in the front, then leapt over the seat to attack the fourth man.

"Ernie—finish them!" Lambert yelled as he worked his struggling adversary into a head lock.

Colon had already stabbed the fifth man, who had tried to run from the car. When Lambert and Weyers had immobilized their opponents, the American pushed his blade between each man's ribs in turn.

It was over in seconds. Panting, Lambert surveyed the carnage. "To hell with the invasion," he said. "Let's stay here and liberate Algeria ourselves."

"Only a Frenchman would call French Algeria liberated," Weyers said breathlessly.

"You're one to talk," Lambert sneered. "How

many South African blacks can even *spell* the word liber—"

"Enough of this," Ogan interrupted. He had drawn his own knife, and now put it away. "You did well, but don't get cocky. These men were green; the rest won't be."

"True. They'll be red," Lambert said. "Bright red."

Weyers retrieved his knife and wiped in on a victim's tunic. "Well, at least now we won't have to walk to town."

Livingston sheathed his own dagger. "Sorry, but I don't think we should take the car."

"Why not?" Ogan asked. "No one will think to look out here for the bodies. And the jeep may save us a night's walk if the farm is very far. We can always ditch it in the country."

"But someone will still miss the soldiers."

"And if we just *leave* the vehicle, the men will be missed *and* found."

"Not if there's an accident, one that burns seven bodies beyond recognition."

Lambert nodded appreciatively. "Six men dating one girl. *C'est magnifique!*"

Livingston pointed behind them. "We can bring the jeep to the rocks, put all the bodies together, and torch the whole shebang. After the explosion, no one will be able to tell that these men didn't just rack the thing up."

"An explosion," Ogan said. "A beacon bringing them right to where we landed."

"Not at all. We cover our tracks and walk back in the surf. One man stays behind until we're well away, blows the car, then takes the long way, over the dunes, so the enemy won't spot him. Case'll be closed. It isn't by the book," Livingston added, "but now we don't really have a choice. It'd be reckless to leave two men behind."

The sergeant major chewed on his lower lip. He looked at the others and nodded. They began loading the bodies back into the car.

As Livingston turned to go, Ogan grabbed his arm. "Your points are well taken, but in the future I'd ask you to present them to me in private."

"Begging your pardon, I did what I thought was expedient."

"Nonetheless, I won't have my authority undermined in front of the men. If there is a next time, you're to take me discreetly aside. Is that understood?"

Livingston hesitated, then nodded slowly.

"I do have a question, though, Livingston."

"Yes?"

"For my own reference. How did you know those soldiers *weren't* on leave?"

"The Germans know there's a big push coming. They're also flying missions over the desert each day. There's no way they would give mechanics leave, not now. I'd say that's also what made our friends suspicious of us—the fact that we're mechanics who were freed up for mine-laying detail."

Ogan nodded and thanked him, after which the two men helped the others stack the bodies on the seats. Lambert drove back to the rocks while the others got on their hands and knees and dragged driftwood behind them to smooth over their tracks.

Livingston used his dagger to cup up one of the seats. "Sergeant, how about me staying behind and setting the fire."

"No. You speak the language better than any of us. I want you with me."

"That's the point. If I'm caught, I can tell them *something*—"

"That's an order, Livingston. Private Colon will stay. He's more than able to take care of himself."

Colon looked up at Livingston and nodded. Livingston turned away.

"All right, Private," Ogan said. "Give us until 0330, then light it. We'll meet you—Lambert, where?"

"In the Casbah . . . the ancient section. That old mosque we were told about. The Germans would have no reason to be there."

"Good. Now let's move out."

The foursome headed for the water, Weyers wiping out their tracks behind them.

Despite the lateness of the hour, the streets of the city of 300,000 were far from deserted. Though lighting street lamps wasn't permitted— illuminating the streets would have made a night-time bombing raid easier—soldiers and natives alike carried shielded lanterns that cast a dull orange glow through narrow slits.

The men had left the beach to keep from being noticed; Ogan didn't want anyone to see them there shortly before there was an explosion. The large Weyers, in particular, was just distinctive enough to be remembered. Taking to the hills, they had come into the city via the Rue Mohammed Zekkal, which meandered north toward the heart of the city. They had stayed to the side streets, walking nearly four kilometers toward the docks just east of the Casbah.

The tension between Ogan and Livingston had been palpable during the hour-long trek; even the normally talkative Lambert had had little to say. But when they entered the Casbah, the mission

took priority, and each man was alert and undis-
tracted.

"Lambert, you've been here before," Ogan said.
"Take over."

The Frenchman stepped in front and led the others into the quarter that had been the heart of the
region's commerce for countless centuries.

The group stayed off the broad Rue Amar Ali
and Rue Abderahmane, which bordered the city
on the east. Those were the roads used by the Germans to move between their barracks at the docks,
the southern hills, and the aerodrome beyond. The
going here was slow, if fascinating.

In maps, the Moslem sector, the Casbah, had reminded Livingston of a cracked windshield: small,
jagged streets running this way and that up the
slopes that surrounded the city. On the ground,
the impression was that there were no streets at
all—just turn after sharp turn. Above them, the
sky was blotted out by the second floors of countless tenements, overhangs that were supported by
heavy wooden struts. Lanterns were hung beneath
these, invisible from above: in these spots of light,
children darted through the crowd of Arabs,
Frenchmen, and German soldiers, playing soccer
with garbage stuffed inside paper bags. A few
youngsters openly picked the pockets of Frenchmen too drunk to notice.

Weyers whispered to Lambert that he was surprised none of the natives seemed to mind the
presence of the Germans. "If this were Pretoria or
Johannesburg or Cape Town, the tads would be
throwing garbage at them, not playing with it."

"Perhaps," Lambert said, "but the city has
known many masters since the Cretan sailors first
landed here. As for the Arabs, they just don't
worry about what happens from day to day or

even year to year. It's like each small street: The Nazis are just another turn they have to endure to get wherever they're going."

"Which is?" Livingston asked.

"Paradise. Eternity. "There won't be any Nazis or Romans or Vandals there—"

"Or French," Weyers pointed out.

"Most certainly not the French," Lambert said proudly. "So why should they care who rules them *now*?"

"The partisans do," Ogan pointed out.

"True, but those are people who have benefited from the prosperity and the rebuilding and the wine that the French brought when they took charge over a century ago. The partisans are less religious and patriotic than they are capitalistic."

Despite the darkness, Livingston could still make out the many sights of the Casbah; because of the darkness, the ghosts of countless centuries seemed to be there still, hiding in the shadows of the old mansions and mosques. The magnificent Djemaa Ali Bitchin, which had been built by an Italian pirate who had converted to Islam. The palace Khedaodj El Amia, a Turkish palace that the French had made their first town hall. Dar Mustapha Pasha and Dar Ahmed, two magnificent estates. In America, buildings were old if they dated to the Revolutionary War. Here, they would be recent history. He could understand why ten or twenty or even one hundred years mattered little to these people.

Though the many commercial establishments were shut, from the ever-present bookstalls to the flower shops, sidewalk cafés were still open, catering not only to those officers with passes but also to the French who remained to run the economy and the figurehead government. Lambert was openly distressed to note that regardless of how the Arabs felt, none of the Frenchmen seemed to mind the German presence. Many were chatting amiably with the Nazis and even laughing. But Lambert didn't stay angry; he was distracted by the prostitutes standing in many doorways and by the eroded figures clandestinely hawking opium and hashish from other dark niches.

He sighed as they turned toward the piers that lined the half-moon-shaped bay. "What a place to be if we weren't working."

"You'd crap yourself up with these things?" Weyers asked.

"In a minute."

"And kill yourself? Or go crazy?"

Lambert looked at him. "Is what we're doing now any safer?"

"Maybe not, but at least it's for a reason."

"So are women and smoke. And the reason is to enjoy life. My father was the healthiest man I've ever known, until Bedouins cut off his hands, hung him upside down in a well, and allowed him to bleed to death."

There was no further conversation as the men walked through the outermost reaches of the Casbah. When the strong odor of the fish market announced that they were near the docks, Ogan tapped Lambert on the shoulder.

"The kiosk is supposed to be right behind the warehouse by the southernmost dock. Do you know where that is?"

"Yes. Under the pipes they use to pump the wine into the ships. They keep the stands and a few shops open for the sailors and stevedores who work at night."

Weyers was shaking his head. "The nomads did that to your father? Why?"

"Because they didn't think the French had any business meddling in their affairs. That's why Hitler spent years sending emissaries to them, bribing them, before he dared move his armies into the area. There aren't many of the vermin, but they aren't people you'd want to cross."

The men fell silent as they left the old section of the city. They crept ahead in the shadows of the warehouses, ducking behind cars or trucks whenever sentries walked by. The French had recently done a great deal of modernization in the harbor, profiting enormously from exports; the Germans were now using the docks and warehouses to store matériel for the North African campaigns.

"Partisans frequently try to set fires at the docks," Lambert whispered as they neared the corner of the last warehouse. "In the two years that the Germans have been here, they've executed over forty Frenchmen."

"We'll nail an extra forty of them for that," Weyers promised as Ogan waved them into silence.

When they reached the edge of the building, Ogan went to the corner and peered around. There were no sentries; just the kiosk, open, a lantern glowing dully within. The only persons about were a pair of sailors chatting with the owner.

Delphine Dupre.

Ogan turned back and nodded. The men rounded the corner, talking in loud voices about who had drunk more wine at the café.

The sailors moved away as they approached. Smiling, Ogan leaned against the cylindrical stand.

"I wonder, miss, if you have more than just newspapers here."

"That depends on what you are looking for."

"A magazine," he said. "*Doc Savage.*"

The young woman smiled and reached below the counter. "It so happens I have that title. Do you read French?"

"*I* can," Lambert said, stepping forward. "*Je vous aime beaucoup, mon cherie, et—*"

"Kill it," Ogan said as he accepted the magazine. "Is there anything in particular you'd like us to read?"

"An advertisement on page eighty. I believe you will find it most . . ."

Her words were cut off by an explosion down the beach. Almost at once, the lanterns were doused and sirens sounded. Infantrymen rushed from the hotels that had been taken over by the military, assembling in the streets to await further orders.

Delphine seemed alarmed. "What is it?"

"Don't worry," Ogan said. "It's ours."

"But why?"

Livingston stepped over. "Just a distraction." He turned to Ogan. "Can I see you for a moment?"

"Pardon?" Ogan's expression was incredulous.

"I want to show you something . . . over here."

Excusing himself, Ogan followed Livingston to the warehouse wall. When they stopped, Ogan could barely contain his anger.

"Damn it, what the *hell* is so important that—"

"Those men." He pointed to the civilian sailors, who stood smoking at the end of the dock. "They're what's important."

"Are you *mad*? They're so far off they couldn't hear us if we were shouting!"

"I don't mean that. Look at their shoes."

Ogan's expression shaded to puzzlement. Pretending to glance at the freighter behind them, he stole a look at the men.

"Short boots," he murmured.

"Lace-up ankle boots, to be precise. Dockworkers don't wear those. Members of the Afrika Korps do."

Ogan rubbed the back of his neck. "Shit."

"Maybe they were trying to pump her ... or maybe she's in with them, which would explain how they nailed Barker."

"If that's true, why aren't they doing the same to us?"

"How do you know they won't? Delphine didn't know where or when we were coming in. She didn't even know how many of us there'd be. They might have been expecting only a man or two."

Ogan opened the thick magazine. He glanced at a map that had been sketched on the advertisement. There was an X at the end of a road that wound through the hills. "The farm. Christ, even that may have been compromised. No explosives."

"It's possible."

Ogan swore again. "I'm sorry. You were right. I don't understand how or why, but one of our two contacts must be bad."

"We can figure out which one later. The question is, what do you want to do about it?"

The sergeant major thought for a moment. "Lose ourselves. I'll go back to Delphine and stall there. You take Weyers and go to the mosque. Lambert and I will keep an eye on these men; if one of them tries to follow you, that'll prove you're right and we'll take him."

Livingston nodded, then casually called Weyers over.

Lambert stepped away from the window when Ogan returned.

"What is it?" Delphine asked.

"Nothing you'd want to hear about," Ogan said. "There were some women back there . . . he wanted to know if we had time to—"

"I'd better go with them," Lambert said. He started out. "Those men don't speak French and—"

Ogan grabbed his jacket sleeve. "They'll be fine. We have work to do."

Ogan's hard gaze told Lambert that there was no debating the point. The Frenchman leaned against the kiosk, his arms across his chest as he watched his comrades disappear down the dark Avenue du 1 Novembre.

Ogan watched the sailors from the corner of his eye. "Mademoiselle Dupre, there's one thing more I'd like to ask you. Have you any idea how the Germans knew that Harold Barker was coming in, or"—he hesitated, swallowed hard—"whether or not he's still alive?"

"The chances are good that he's still alive. Partisans are executed at once, but persons who possess information are usually kept alive and questioned over a period of two or three weeks. Most often they die from the interrogation before they can be shot."

"Thank God."

"How they found out about him," she went on, "I've no idea. It was a shock to me when Chadli mentioned it. As for his whereabouts, the Nazis have been using an old prison roughly a kilometer south of the city. All captives are taken there."

One of the sailors threw his cigarette in the bay and headed in the direction Livingston and Weyers had taken. The other man walked in the opposite direction, toward a row of cars that had lined up to take soldiers down to the beach. The headlights of each was covered with cat's-eye shield, which cast only a sliver of light ahead. From above, they would be virtually invisible.

Ogan resisted the urge to put his knife to the woman's throat and demand to know whether she'd turned on them. Instead, he tucked the magazine under his arm and smiled politely.

"Thanks for your help," he said. "If there's anything else, we'll let you know."

"I will do whatever I can. Monsieur Abdelghani, at the farm, will also do anything to help. Do not hesitate to ask him."

Ogan promised that he would, then walked briskly toward the Casbah. In the press of soldiers roused by the explosion, no one paid him or Lambert any attention.

"Why the rush?" Lambert said.

"Those two sailors were Germans," he replied, "probably military intelligence."

"Then . . . my darling betrayed us?"

"It appears so."

Lambert whistled. "I don't believe it. I'm a better judge of women than that."

"Everyone makes mistakes."

Lambert muttered deprecations while he and Ogan scanned the now crowded street for the sailor.

"You two! *Halten!*"

Lambert and Ogan turned. Together, they stared into the grim face of the second sailor and a detachment of soldiers.

"Did you think to get away?" the sailor demanded. "Raise your hands, or I'll shoot you here."

The men did as they were told. As the sailor searched them for weapons, Ogan was hardly surprised to note that, back at the kiosk, Delphine was nowhere to be seen.

Chapter Six

The mosque was open but musty, rank with the odor of men and the ages. It wasn't as grand as some of the other mosques in the Lower Casbah, but because it was smaller it would be easier for the two men to watch the entire building. There was no one else inside, and Livingston directed Weyers to an archway that led to one of the two slender, octagonal minarets. The American concealed himself just inside the other passage.

Nearly a quarter of an hour passed before anyone entered. It was too early for Colon to have arrived, and Livingston peeked out cautiously. In the faint orange light of a brazier, he saw the newcomer.

A German soldier.

Livingston watched closely; he held his breath until the man turned and went into the street. Was it just a routine check, or were they casing the place before moving in?

The American's palms grew warm. Perspiration beaded his forehead and dripped into his eyes, stinging them. More minutes passed. How many, he had no idea; his perception of time became badly skewed the longer he waited.

Finally, two soldiers entered, with more purpose than the first man. They were followed by two more, and then one of the sailors. All had their guns drawn.

Livingston decided that they must have checked other likely buildings on the street, the cafés and the brothels, before coming here. He backed up as the five man fanned through the small mosque.

There was a dark, circular staircase behind him. To get to him on top of it, they'd have to come up single file, unable to set up a crossfire. He began walking backward, slowly, making his way up.

The sailor stepped back. The lights of the passing cars revealed four soldiers, each holding a pistol; the sailor, too, was armed. There was a smirk on his lips that were too small for his lantern jaw.

"The explosion," he said. "Was it yours? Something to lure us out to the beach?"

"I don't know what you're talking about."

"Of course not. You're from Britain. I think—although your accent is commendable. And you're here for sabotage, like the fool who came before you."

Ogan's jaw grew rigid. It was all he could do to keep from throwing himself at the German.

"I must admit, though, I expected something more subtle than an explosion. Still, I suppose that with the area cleared of soldiers, you'd have been free to sabotage a warehouse or two, perhaps get on board one of the ships. Not bad for a night's work." He glanced at his watch. "We must go. But before we do, let us be a civilized as possible. I am *Oberstleutnant* Hauptmann. What are your names?"

Ogan and Lambert said nothing. The officer pressed his P.38 to Ogan's side. "Very well. You can tell me your names willingly or unwillingly, it makes no difference. But I assure you, you *will* tell me who you are—and why you were sent."

Ogan studied the men. The street was all but deserted now, the last of the cars having departed. There was no way he and Lambert could hope to get away.

He silently cursed himself for having ignored this man to follow the other. He hoped only that Livingston and Weyers were faring better.

Passing the minaret window, Livingston reached the top of the first story. He stopped there, just below the balcony, and dragged his sleeve across his eyes as he listened.

If he were right, two men would ascend each balcony while the sailor waited downstairs. If not, if they were as inexperienced as the kids on the beach and were searching one tower at a time, either he or Weyers would have to take them all. He wondered what the hell had delayed Ogan.

Livingston heard smart new boots squeak below. Ogan be damned, they were going to have to handle this themselves. The American cocked the pistol, using his tunic to muffle the sound.

The soldier climbed the steps. There was a second set of boots behind him; just that and no more. The group had divided.

Livingston crouched. The men were just beyond the turn in the stairwell. He wouldn't fire until the first man was in full view.

Suddenly, there was a scream from the other minaret, followed by a single shot and shouts from below.

"Up here! They're in this one!"

Livingston swore as the men below him turned and ran. He pursued them as quietly as possible, reaching the base of the stairs as they bolted through the mosque. He hoped the scream hadn't come from Weyers.

Some plan, he thought as he ran. They'd been ashore just two hours, yet not one thing had gone right. He vowed that if he survived, he'd kill Ogan, Escott, Sweet, and Captain Thorpe in that order.

In the dim light of the single torch on the wall, Livingston saw a soldier sprawled dead across the last few steps of the other minaret. The sergeant was relieved. There had been only one shot, and he didn't imagine the scream had come from the burly South African. Livingston watched as the two remaining soldiers and the sailor ran to the minaret.

The American raised his pistol, but before he could fire, three more soldier ran in. They saw him and shouted; with an oath, Livingston shot at them and ducked behind the doorway.

"Get him!"

The sailor's yell was followed by footsteps, which stopped just around the corner from where Livingston was standing. The American's heart pushed against his throat. There were a million ways they could get him: force of numbers, tear gas, even sending someone through the minaret window. But there was only one way he could get them, and that was if they were stupid enough to walk right in.

He waited. And prayed.

And God heard him. The holy place reverberated with gunfire.

The shooting lasted just a few seconds, and it all seemed to come from one place: the front doorway. When it was over, Livingston cautiously poked his head into the room.

And smiled.

"Sweet, *sweet* Jesus."

Colon grinned. "Having some trouble here?"

Weyers came out from behind the other archway. "Ernesto! By God, you're as lovely a sight as these two blue eyes have *ever* seen."

Livingston ran forward. "Likewise. For some reason, our cavalry never arrived."

"And they won't arrive, either."

The sergeant stopped short. "What do you mean?"

"Lambert and our commander had Heinie problems. When I was on the way in, they were on the way out—in the back of a half-track surrounded by soldiers."

"Which way were they headed?"

"Back toward the beach."

"A half-track should be easy to spot. Let's go, in case they're still in the city." Livingston pointed to the other side of the mosque. "We'll leave by the back, in case there're more goons where these came from."

The men jogged across the room and, after checking the narrow street, hurried out.

The odor of sewage was strong as they ran beside an open drain that had been cut ages before in the middle of the road. Passing the far minaret, Livingston was surprised to see a dead soldier lying in the street. Two elderly Algerians came toward them; both casually stepped over the soldier's body.

"What happened to him?" Livingston asked.

"He fell," Weyers said. "For an old trick, that is. I scuffed the soot on the window ledge. When he looked out, I gave him a boot."

"I never heard of that one before."

"You never had to run from Pretoria lawmen when you were a boy. We usually stopped short of knocking them out windows, but we made them think that was where *we'd* gone."

There were shouts in the mosque, but by the time soldiers came running through the backdoor, the three men had lost themselves in the depths of the Casbah.

Though the men spent the better part of the night wandering the streets of Algiers, they were unable to find Ogan and Lambert. It was nearly dawn when they paused in a small square to draw water from a crumbling well.

Weyers washed his face in the warm, silty water. "Now what?"

"What about the airfield?" Colon asked Livingston. "Do you think they might have taken them there?"

"It's possible, but why take the security risk? If I were the Krauts, I'd take them as far from the base as possible." Livingston splashed his face with water from the wooden bucket. "There's got to be a prison compound somewhere in the city, a place where they take all their prisoners for interrogation. And I'm willing to bet our friend the farmer knows where it is."

"Sure," said Weyers, "if we can find him."

"I saw the map. We can head to the farm and reconnoiter, see what kind of arms we have at our disposal. Even if we can't get to Ogan and Lambert, we still have a job to do."

Colon agreed at once. Weyers was uneasy.

"If that Dupre woman's as Kraut as you say, there's no way the weapons'll be there."

"It's possible, but we can't afford not to check.

Especially if the farmer's the only one who knows where we can find Ogan and Lambert.''

Weyers reluctantly agreed, and gathering up their gear, the men walked down the dusty road into the bare, silent hills.

It was ironic, Ogan thought as he marched around the small cell. He'd run a prison, and now he was being held in one. His entire combat career had consisted of rowing across a small stretch of sea; not something to boast about to his son—assuming he ever got back to England. At this point, that seemed doubtful.

The prison was more or less as he had anticipated: a small, stuffy structure of white, clay-covered stone, with just over a dozen crowded cells. Each cell was a small cubicle with a heavy door. There were no windows, save for the short, thick bars at the top of the door.

As he was led to his cell, Ogan was unable to determine whether Barker was among the prisoners. Not that it mattered. He'd be lucky to find a way out himself, let alone help anyone else. He knew he'd be lucky if he were even thinking clearly after a few hours in enemy hands.

Ogan had never really wondered how he would bear up under torture. It wasn't a circumstance he ever thought would arise. The confusion he felt about this was complicated by a weakness in his hands and knees, a recurrence of the paralysis he'd experienced in London—the fear that he was going to fail his friend. He hoped only that anger would harden him. Not just anger over what Delphine Dupre had done to him and to the Allies, but what she'd done to Barker.

The key rattled in the door. It swung open and the square-jawed Hauptmann entered. Only now, instead of a pistol, he carried a riding crop; instead of a sailor's suit, he wore the uniform of an SS *oberstleutnant*. Behind him, a uniformed aide entered with a lantern, which he hung from a hook on the wall.

The German studied Ogan in the light. "Are you feeling any more cooperative than before?"

"I am Kenneth Ogan, sergeant major, serial number—"

The officer held up a gloved hand. "The serial number is not necessary, Sergeant Major Ogan. We are not dogs, we are men. *Responsible* men. And I have come to tell you that if, at any time, you wish to leave this . . . this kennel, simply call out."

Ogan turned away.

"You must see that your mission has failed, Sergeant Major, but don't feel shame in that. You were *sacrificed* by uncaring superiors in a futile undertaking. Cooperate with us. We know that there are others in your group, and we also know that they are in the hills. We are searching for them, and soon your entire team will be in our custody. *Someone* will tell us what we wish to know. Ask yourself, under the circumstances, if silence is wise. Is a doomed invasion worth suffering for . . . worth dying for?"

Ogan's hands were shaking and he clasped them behind him. "Kenneth Ogan, sergeant major, serial number 32862746—"

"Enough!" The officer motioned to his aide and the man retrieved the lantern." If you wish to behave like a dog, then you will be whipped like a dog. But first, you will listen to the others, Sergeant Major. We will see if they are as stubborn or as *foolish* as you!"

Ogan swallowed an oath as the men left him

once again in darkness—but not in silence. From down the corridor, from the first muted crack of the crop, the utter desolation and guilt that welled up in him were worse than any pain he'd ever felt.

The first light of dawn revealed a sight that Livingston had half anticipated.

The men had ascended the western hills, which formed a huge amphitheater around the city. Despite everything that had happened, the silhouette of Algiers against the bay had taken the men's breath away. There were bell-shaped towers, white boxlike buildings, large paneless windows through which the sparkling harbor shone, and ornate temples and mausoleums. A cloud of red dust had just begun to form over the rooftops, kicked up as people shuffled to the markets and shops. The haze had diffused the morning light, and it had been a moment of extreme beauty and serenity.

They'd climbed, avoiding the quiet roads that wound through villas and gardens, ancient churches with their silver cupolas and weatherworn statues, and houses that clung precariously to the sides of rocky cliffs. They'd stuck to the scrubby paths where only an occasional hut, Roman ruin, or bleating goat were to be found. Because it was the coastal roads that led to the aerodrome, there was no enemy traffic here.

Now the sense of serenity was gone, replaced by desolation. Lying on their bellies at the edge of a small patch of wild grass, they looked down through binoculars at a clearing where several hills met. There, in a pale gray pile, lay the charred ruins of a man's life—along with the wreck of their own hopes.

"Whoever turned us in also ratted on the chicken rancher," Weyers complained.

Livingston glanced around. The barn had been burned to the ground, nothing remaining but ash and charred timbers. Looking at a stretch of field on the far side of the property, the sergeant saw several holes. "I've got some more bad news. It looks like the Germans also got the weapons that were stashed here."

"It's amazing the damage one rotten apple can do," Weyers said.

"There's nothing lower than a collaborator," Colon added. "God help that French bitch if I ever get my hands on her."

"You won't," Livingston assured him. "And if we don't make it back to England, chances are good the SIS will never suspect that she's . . ."

Livingston bit off the rest of the sentence as Colon suddenly rose and darted back up through the tall grass.

"Hey, what are you doing?"

The soldier didn't acknowledge him. He continued on, running into the glare of the sun and disappearing over a rise. Livingston crouched and watched as Colon ran onto the road that cut through the hills.

Weyers squat beside Livingston. "What in God's name does he think he's doing?"

"Going around to the other side, it looks like." Livingston trained his binoculars on the hill across from them. He saw the thick grasses—and the glint of reflected sunlight. "I'll be damned, there's someone there." He laid the binoculars down. "Cover me."

"What are you going to do?"

"Keep that son of a bitch's attention so Colon can get behind him."

"Using yourself as bait?"

"You got a better idea?"

Rising, Livingston started moving toward the burned-out remains of the farm. He walked stooped over, weaving from side to side so as not to make an easy target. But he made certain he was visible. The man mustn't turn around.

It was just under two hundred meters to the foot of the hill. Livingston was nearly at the bottom when he heard a man scream on the opposite hill. He stopped and looked over as Colon rose. The private had his knife to the man's throat; the captive's arm was twisted behind his back.

The man was not German. His complexion was swarthy, his clothing consisting of a dirty black robe and a matching turban. There was a British rifle slung over his shoulder, a short-magazine Lee-Enfield. Continuing down the hill, Livingston met Colon and his prisoner on the other side of the rubble.

"Good work." Livingston took the Algerian's rifle and Colon released him. The man threw himself at Livingston's feet, his hands locked in supplication.

"I beg of you," he said in broken German, "don't hurt me! I have been out of my head since I lost my farm . . . but I'm better now. Truly, I am."

"Was this your farm?" Livingston asked.

"Yes . . . yes!"

"Who burned it?"

"Other soldiers. They came two nights ago."

"And you've been hiding here, ever since?"

"I had nowhere else to go—"

"You weren't waiting for anyone? Family?"

The Algerian looked up, his dark brow knit with pain. "I have no family, *sadiq*. They are dead."

Livingston knelt and looked into the man's eyes.

"My only other question, then, is—did you manage to salvage any of the explosives, Chadli?"

The man's face hardened. He looked from Livingston to Colon then back again. "You are Force Five?"

Livingston nodded.

"Bah! I should have known!" He gestured at Colon. "This man looks German like I do, and that is not very much." He turned on the private and rubbed the arm that had been twisted behind him. "You nearly caused a dislocation, you know. In the future I would be very careful if I were you, sneaky one!"

"Oh?"

"Oh! You think I jest? Will you say 'oh' if I'm forced to feed you your testicles?"

Colon looked as though he were about to slug the short, thin man. Livingston cautioned him with a glance, then handed Chadli his rifle. That seemed to calm him somewhat; the Algerian suddenly turned toward Colon, aimed the rifle, and fired. Well behind the American, a hanging vine snapped in two.

"What the hell—!"

"Let that be a lesson to you! Chadli Abdelghani is a force with which to be reckoned!"

Colon started toward him. "Chadli Abdelghani is going to be an *ex*-force in two shakes of a—"

Livingston put his hand on Colon's chest. "This is getting to be a habit, Private. We're on the same team, remember?"

"I've slugged teammates before."

"I'm sure. But there's more at stake than a touchdown. Why don't you let me handle this?"

Colon turned away; Chadli stood exhaling loudly, like a bull.

"You pull a stunt like that again," Livingston

said to the Algerian, "and I'll break your goddamn arm. Any questions?"

Chadli shook his head. He poked a blackened slat with his toe. "I'm sorry. I should not have done that. It's been a difficult time and I . . . I was just, as you say, letting off steam."

"The private accepts your apology, and he's sorry he roughed you up," Livingston said. He glowered at Colon. "Isn't he?"

Colon nodded grudgingly, then sat down and jabbed at the sand with his knife.

"Now what about the explosives?" Livingston asked. "Did the Germans get them all?"

"The Germans," the Algerian said. "Let me tell you something about the rancid Germans. It wasn't enough that they shot my wife—a good woman. When you looked into her beautiful green eyes, you saw only love there. And my sons . . . my babies." He squeezed back tears. "Now they take what little I have left. My farm, my few possessions, my chickens." He looked up, his dark eyes grim. "No, *sadiq*. The Germans did not get the explosives. I would die before I'd let that happen."

Livingston smiled and clapped the small Algerian on the arms. "Good man!"

"*Shoukran.*" Chadli touched his fingers to his lips and bowed slightly. "Thank you. But I'm just a simple man who applied good sense. After the others were captured in the hills, I knew that the Nazis would destroy this place looking for our explosives and weapons. So I buried several bags in the hills." He swept his hand over the shallow holes. "These represent what I left behind for them to find. There remain more than enough to blow the devils and their aircraft back to Berlin."

Even Colon smiled. "Now you're talkin'."

Livingston called Weyers to join them. When he

arrived, the sergeant instructed the big South African to remain behind in case a German patrol showed up. He readily agreed, returning to his post as Chadli took the men into the hills.

The armada was one of the largest ever assembled. Even after six days at sea, traveling a circuitous, northeastern route to fool the enemy as to their real destination, Rear Admiral H. Kent Hewitt was both awed and humble to be commanding the fleet ferrying the 35,000 men of Major General Patton's Western Task Force four thousand miles across the Atlantic to Casablanca.

He looked out from the deck of his flagship, the aircraft carrier *USS Ranger*, at 102 ships spread as far as he could see in every direction. The proud ships and the slate gray seas seemed to share the same angry purpose, a surging, forward motion. Both seemed immutable, their surface only hinting at its power.

Despite the size of the undertaking and its importance to American prestige, Hewitt wasn't concerned about the crossing. Nor was he worried about his British counterpart, Admiral Sir Andrew Cunningham, who was commanding the British Mediterranean Fleet—despite the fact that Cunningham was moving two separate convoys through the Mediterranean: 250 merchantmen with 39,000 British and American troops in one, bound for Oran; and 160 Royal Navy ships with 23,000 British troops and 10,000 American troops in the other, headed for Algiers. Though all of them were sailing waters prowled by ships of the Italian and German fleets, the enemy probably would not dare to take on such a large armada.

Hewitt wasn't concerned about the crossings. But once the soldiers hit the beach, they would be open to attack from well-entrenched enemy troops.

Artillery. Tanks.

Planes.

In particular, German spotter planes would report back on the size and exact destination of the incoming fleet, while bombers would wreak havoc on the landing craft and soldiers.

Hewitt had been told that there was a team in Algiers working to sabotage the German aerodromes. With just two days until the landings, he stood alone and silently prayed for the nearly 110,000 men whose lives would depend on the wits and deeds of a handful of brave souls. . . .

Chapter Seven

"Here is where it happened."

Chadli paused, his proud shoulders drooping as the men passed the shell of a farm higher in the hills. One of the walls had countless holes in it, small dark craters fringed with uneven rings of brown.

Dried blood.

"My friend Mohammed raised cows here, and together we would go to the marketplace to sell milk and eggs. We were very clever about it," Chadli said wistfully. "If people wanted only my eggs, we would give them a discount to take his milk as well. And the other way around. Whichever of us made a sale he would not otherwise have made, he would pay half of his profits to the one for whose goods the customer had originally come. Very clever of us, no?"

"Yes." Livingston smiled as they paused before the wall. He noticed that some of the blood seemed fresher than the rest.

Chadli sighed. "We shared many good times. Our children played together and our wives helped one another with their duties. I loved Mohammed as though he were a brother." He pointed toward a ledge overlooking the barn. "I was up there chasing a rabbit for dinner when they came. Mohammed was the last of the Resistance fighters to be executed. The others and their families, his family included, all died before his eyes. My own family"—his voice choked—"my own family was here when the Germans came. I saw them murdered." He raised his eyes to the hill. "Mohammed was stronger than I. He did not weep. I did as I watched it happen ... and then again that night as I opened the pit the Germans had forced peasants to dig for the bodies. I reburied the victims in separate graves and blessed them."

Livingston couldn't imagine living with that kind of pain, that kind of hatred. It would drive him mad to see his family's killers every day and not be able to lash out.

"I'm sorry," was all Livingston could say.

Chadli swallowed hard. "While the killers were checking the bodies, I ran back down the hill. It was dark, and my eyes were blinded by tears, but Allah guided my feet. And when I reached my farm, I dug up the dynamite we had been stealing in small amounts from the Nazis. I hid in the grass and lay beside the explosives as the devils came and burned my farm and dug up the arms I left behind. When they finally left, I moved the explosives to a safer place."

"And you've been waiting for us ever since."

"I have. Despite Mr. Barker's unfortunate capture, I assumed that others would come." Impulsively, Chadli hugged Livingston. "I'm glad you *have* come, for together we will *slay* the demons for what they've done to us. The Koran teaches that it is not honorable to seek vengeance ... but I want these sons of snakes to burn in hell."

"They will," Livingston promised—along with the French girl who had betrayed them and the brave Algerian partisans.

The explosives were buried in a dense wood at the top of the hills, hidden beneath patches of club moss that had been scooped up and replanted. The men dug up more than twenty separate clumps, removing sticks of dynamite from some, hand grenades and pistols from others. All had been wrapped in wax paper to keep them dry.

"Impressive, no?" the Algerian asked.

Livingston said it was. "Except for these," he remarked, examining the guns. "Beretta automatics. Short-round, nine-millimeter—effective only at close range."

Chadli grew indignant. "They worked well for us."

"What did you use them for?"

"Defending the self. In case anyone saw us when we boarded trucks or entered warehouses to steal explosives."

"I see. A question, Chadli. Did you ever work with Mademoiselle Dupré?"

"Delphine? An angel, a true daughter of the Resistance."

"Why do you say that?"

"Because she went with us on *every* mission, whether it was to steal arms or cut telephone wires or obtain maps or intelligence."

"And did you ever see her use one of these?"

"A gun?" Chadli scratched his grizzled cheek. "No, I do not believe I ever saw her kill anyone. But she was seldom required to stand guard, friend Livingston. Delphine was so silent that she was the one who usually went into rooms and conveyances to obtain whatever we needed. Why do you ask these things? Is she in trouble?"

Livingston explained what had happened back at the dock. Chadli listened intently, and when the American was finished, the Algerian shook his head violently.

"I cannot believe what you are telling me. She would never have cooperated with the Nazis. Never!"

"Why not? She wasn't rounded up with the rest of the Resistance fighters."

"She wasn't with us that night. Nor were my comrades questioned about any others. In their haste to be rid of the underground, the Nazis lined them up and shot them. I overheard them say that any partisans who remained would be too frightened to show themselves." He thumped his chest with his fist. "They didn't know that they were talking about me and Delphine. And we're not frightened by them."

"But you haven't spoken to Mademoiselle Dupre since before the executions."

"No. I was waiting in the hills for you."

While they were speaking, Livingston had been replacing the swatches of moss. Colon cushioned the dynamite and potato mashers by wrapping them in the men's civilian clothes, then replaced them in their duffel bags.

Just as they were finishing, the men heard shots. The reports echoed, disguising their point of origin; the three men stood, listening like wary deer. There were more shots, and this time the trio threw the sacks over their shoulders and ran down the slopes toward the sound of the gunfire.

Toward the spot where they'd left Weyers.

The South African was curled behind a small stack of charred wood, all that was left of one wall of Chadli's farmhouse. He knew he couldn't run anywhere from there because there was an open field in every direction; worse, he had no idea what he'd do if any of the soldiers got to the hill behind him.

I'll die, probably, he thought. *Unless they're too damn stupid to think of that.*

He couldn't believe he'd let them sneak up on him like that. At least they'd been overanxious and fired at him before they had a clear shot. By the time they'd fired the second volley, he was already rolling down the hill, a difficult target.

Now that he had a few minutes before they charged or went behind him, he tried to figure out what he'd do.

Weyers didn't even know how many troops there were. He'd only seen two, but there were probably more. The bastards usually traveled in packs, like wolves. He held his pistol tightly, hoped that Livingston hadn't gone so far he wouldn't hear the shots. At least if he could hold out until the other three returned—

A bullet pinged against the wood beside him. Weyers hugged the ground. A second shot struck inches from his feet, but from the other direction. He tucked his feet in tighter.

"Holy mother!"

A voice came from the hill. "Surrender! There is nowhere you can run."

Weyers had only seconds to make a decision. If he tried to shoot in one direction, the man or men on the other side would gun him down. If he sat there, they would probably decide to keep shooting at him just the same. That was the way *he'd* been trained at the #5 SAAF school outside Pretoria: When in doubt, destroy.

There was no choice. He had to buy time, and hope that Livingston could catch up to them, hope that the American would even take the *time* to try and rescue him. If not, he would have to bear up under two days of torture before the Allied landing. From what he'd heard, two days in Nazi hands would feel like two weeks.

Still, as long as he could keep his mouth shut, it was better than dying here.

He tossed his gun well away from the rubble. *"Nicht toten!"* he yelled in broken German as he rose. "Don't kill me!"

Three soldiers came scurrying down the south hill, while another three rose from the grasses on the north side. Weyers was glad he'd opted not to fight. The odds were awful, even by the lopsided standards to which he was accustomed. Reaching him, one of the soldiers put a gun to his back. The others took up positions in front of him.

Like a firing squad.

"Where are your comrades?" the man behind demanded.

"Sorry, mate," Weyers said in Afrikaans, just in case the men understood English. "Don't speak the language."

The soldier cocked his handgun, pressed it to the back of the South African's neck. *"Where are the others?"*

"Nein sprechen!" Weyers repeated, hoping he sounded convincing.

The man behind him hesitated. Weyers squinted into the sun. This part was getting to be old hat. When Rommel had marched into Tobruk in June, and the 6th South African Armoured Car Regiment had been captured, he was certain he was going to be executed right then and there. But the Good Lord had spared him by letting him steal that German cargo plane during the march back west. Spared him . . . not, Weyers believed, to die here, on a desolate hill in Algeria. That made no sense.

It was the last thought the South African had before he felt a pain in the back of his head, and his world went black.

Upon reaching the hills overlooking the clearing, Livingston sent Colon to the northern summit and Chadli to the south. With the Algerian's rifle in hand, he crouched on the eastern hill and kept watch on both sides.

The grasses stirred as the two men moved through them, and Livingston looked, from time to time, at the rubble to make certain no one was hiding inside. He thought he saw blood on the ground near the ruins, but he couldn't be certain.

Livingston hated to waste time reconnoitering, but if anything had happened to Weyers, the perpetrators might still be around.

He was glad he'd taken the precaution.

On the southern ridge, the grasses moved several dozen meters ahead of Chadli. Livingston raised the British rifle. It could be a rabbit. Or Weyers. He waited and watched.

A gun cracked on the northern ridge. Livingston spun around and saw a mass of dark blue green.

Not Weyers's uniform.

He fired and there was a burst of red. The blue green mass disappeared. He swung the gun to the other ridge, heard a scream as Chadli's knife came down. The grasses were motionless on both sides as the men waited. Several minutes passed, and then Chadli rose.

"Come out! There is no one else—"

There was a pop from well down the road that

cut through the western hill; Chadli spun and went down. Swearing, Livingston drew a bead on the cloud of smoke.

It was too far!

He raised his hand slowly, motioning Colon to continue on, then set out in the opposite direction. Within minutes, he'd reached Chadli. The Algerian was squirming and holding his shoulder.

"I—I was impatient, Livingston. I am sorry."

The American examined the wound. Although there was a lot of blood, the bullet had only scraped the flesh. "You'll live, but I've got to leave you here—"

"I understand. Get him—cut the balls off that viper!"

Livingston patted him on the side and continued on.

Logic told him that there would be at least two more men up there, setting up a crossfire on the road. The question was how those men would react now that their comrades had been killed. Would they stay put, flee, or circle back?

Livingston would have liked to hurl one of the hand grenades to smoke the soldiers out. But an explosion might bring more troops, and that was something they couldn't afford.

He continued ahead, crouching low. The spot from which the soldier had fired was nearly fifty meters ahead. He saw no movement, no color but the pale yellow of the grass, but he had to assume the soldiers wouldn't fall back.

Livingston stopped. A twig snapped to the left. Quietly, he undid his holster and removed his pistol. He listened. If someone were stalking him, they were now standing still as well.

The morning had grown warm. Gnats brushed his nose and cheeks, but he didn't swat them away.

Even his breathing was slow, shallow. His legs began to cramp.

Livingston was the first to admit that patience had never been one of his strong suits. He had the feeling that Colon could outwait the dead but, as at the mosque, his own mind rebelled at any delays.

Livingston still held the rifle in his left hand. Flinging it in that direction, he rolled to the right.

There was a single shot—at the rifle. Livingston fired twice at the spot from which the report had come, and the man fell. Then, figuring that the enemy wouldn't fire at his own man, Livingston crawled quickly in that direction. He lay beside the German, who had been hit with both shots, once in the upper arm and once in the hip.

The American looked toward the northern hill. Colon's German didn't shoot back, obviously afraid to reveal his own position. If there were any other soldiers, they, too, held their fire.

As he stared, the sergeant saw something that took him completely by surprise. A thin white cloud of smoke was rising from the grass. Livingston stared as the cloud grew dark, its underbelly licked by orange flames.

Someone began backing away from the blaze and shot through it, toward the west. Livingston wished he knew who it was. Suddenly, on the other side of the flame, a cap was thrown up into the air. It was Colon's, a signal.

It had been the German who fired. Aiming in his direction, Livingston sprayed the area with bullets. There was a moan, then silence. Colon and Livingston waited.

The fire was beginning to spread. Livingston wanted to get away before anyone saw it and reinforcements arrived; obviously, Colon had the same idea.

"Sergeant!"

Livingston cupped a hand over his mouth. "Here!"

"Cover me. I'm coming over."

Retrieving the rifle, Livingston swept slowly across the hills. "Now!"

Colon ran down and crossed the clearing. There was no further gunfire and, scurrying up the hill, he knelt beside Livingston.

"The fire was a damn good idea." Livingston said.

"Thanks. How's Chadli?"

Livingston told him as, crouching, they headed to where he'd left the wounded German. To their surprise, they found Chadli lying on top of him, grinning; the German's throat had been cut from ear to ear. Livingston didn't even try to conceal his disgust.

"What is wrong?" the Algerian asked.

"This! Christ, it wasn't necessary."

"No? Did *you* not just kill two men?"

"They were immediate threats. This man was already down!"

"Down or up, his people have killed my people. He deserved to die."

Livingston didn't wish to debate the point. He looked uneasily at the growing fire, then down at the German. Finally, he regarded Chadli. "Can you walk?"

The Algerian rose unsteadily. "I can. But I have another suggestion."

"Which is?"

"I can also hide. And given my condition, that would seem to make greater sense."

Livingston considered this. The truth was,

Chadli *would* slow them down. "Will you be all right?"

"I've been wounded before, Livingston. There is a river not far from the graves. I can minister to myself, and at the same time reflect on what needs to be done."

"I don't like leaving a wounded man alone, but there doesn't seem to be much choice."

"None."

Livingston handed Chadli his gear. "Any idea where they may have taken Weyers?"

"There is only one place: the prison. All captives are taken to it."

"How do we get there?"

"Go back down the road ... head to where it forks, then walk for a kilometer. The prison stands upon a cliff overlooking the sea."

Livingston motioned and Colon also handed Chadli his gear. "We'll come back for these and for you," said Livingston to Chadli. "In the meantime, don't try and execute anymore Germans. If the three of us are all that's left, I can't afford to lose you."

"As long as there are Germans there will be Chadli," he said as Livingston and Colon started toward the clearing.

Chapter Eight

Ogan had no idea how much time had passed. It seemed like an hour or two; there had been enough time for him to go around the cell once, thoroughly, trying to find a weak spot. He'd bloodied his fingers in an effort to push the bolts from the hinges of the door, and rubbed his knuckles raw digging at the hard earth at the foot of the outside wall.

Though he kept busy, it wasn't possible to ignore what was happening down the hall. Lambert—assuming it was the Frenchman—didn't scream. He was a proud and resilient man, and it would take more than the snap of a crop to break him. Soon, though, the Germans would go to greater extremes. Despite the confident words of Hauptmann, knowing that an invasion was imminent and being able to counter it were two very different things. The Nazis had no idea that he and Lambert knew few details, and would push until they broke . . . or died.

The flogging stopped.

It was his turn. He was shaking and hated him-

self for it; he breathed deeply in an effort to calm
himself down.

There were footsteps in the hallway. Keys jan-
gled, several doors creaked open and closed, and
he rose as his own door swung open. Hauptmann
walked in, a smug look on his face and a bloodied
riding crop slung casually across his shoulder.

The officer stepped aside as an aide hoisted a
lantern to the hook. Then something was pushed
into the cell. It collided with Ogan and slumped
facedown to the floor.

The mass was a body—naked, its flesh lacerated, its limbs twisted.

Ogan's stomach began to boil. The body was too
big to be Lambert. Gently, the Englishman turned
it over.

And wailed.

The SS officer smiled crookedly. "I take it you
know him."

Ogan was unaware that the officer had spoken.
He sat on the hard floor, looked from the body to
the blood on his hands. He closed his fingers
slowly. It hadn't been Lambert they were beating.
Dear God, it was Barker!

When Hauptmann's aide came and dragged the
body out, Ogan didn't even try to stop him. Everything seemed surreal, dreamlike.

Barker! God, what did they do to him?

Still wearing a lopsided smile, the SS officer
went over and retrieved the lantern. Ogan remained on his knees gazing blankly out the door.

"He is still alive, Sergeant Major. If you cooperate, he and the rest of your party will remain
alive and unharmed. If not . . ."

The German didn't bother finishing. He stepped
from the cell and the door was locked, once more

leaving Ogan in darkness. He sunk down, his head in his hands.

Barker.

Livingston had been right, of course. He hadn't come to Algeria just to blow up planes. He'd come hoping to find out what had happened to his friend; hoping to rescue him, if possible. Now that he knew Barker was alive, Ogan wondered how he could possibly let him die. He didn't know much about the invasion, but if what he knew could be bartered for Barker's safety . . .

No!

He could never commit treason. What kind of a life would he or Barker or Cindy have then? Yet, what kind of a life would he have knowing he'd let Barker die?

Ogan held the sides of his head, tried to press away the pain and doubt. As in London, during that target practice, he couldn't marshal his thoughts. Things had been so much clearer when he was *running* a prison. In Coventry there were rules, and if they weren't followed, the prisoners were disciplined. The rules here weren't so explicit. And the stakes . . .

Ogan finally slumped down and, unable to move, he sat and pondered whether betraying a nation or betraying a friend was the more heinous crime.

From behind a crumbling wall, Livingston used his binoculars to study the small, boxlike prison. It sat alone on a cliff. A dirt road led right to the front door; uneven hills sloped away steeply on either side. Behind it was a sheer drop of some three hundred feet to the ocean.

There were a pair of guards at the door, which was the only entrance on this side. To the right of the building sat the half-track that Colon had seen take Ogan and Lambert away.

Colon was studying the terrain with his own glasses. "Are you sure you don't want to try and bluff our way in?"

Livingston shook his head. "They'll ask to see our papers. Someone may notice we come from the same unit as Weyers, in which case we're cooked."

"If we come straight down the road, they're gonna nail us anyway. Even if we wait until night, there's no way to get close enough without being seen."

Livingston sat down behind the ancient stone wall. "Not necessarily. There's a way we can do it, but only at night."

Colon asked how. Livingston told him. The private's eyes rolled back.

"You aren't serious. Even if it had a snowball's chance of workin', Weyers may be dead by then."

"He's a tough monkey. It'll take more than an afternoon to break him."

"What about the others? If Ogan and Lambert are there, what if they *talk*?"

"And what if *we're* caught? I've got more confidence in them being able to keep their mouths shut than our ability to take that prison in broad daylight. Besides, time's running out. If we don't get a look at that damn airfield and make some plans, we'll do a piss-poor job when we have to hit it."

Colon shook his head. "I don't like the idea of leaving them in enemy hands." He looked from Livingston to the prison. "Anyway, you aren't in charge of this operation. You can't order me to leave my buddies."

"I still have rank, soldier."

"That ain't gonna help you here, Sergeant."

Livingston remained calm. "Maybe not, but splitting up won't help *either* of us." He put the binoculars away. "You do what you want. I'm going to the damn airfield to do the job we were *sent* here for."

Colon glanced back as Livingston rose and started toward the road. Sneering, Colon reluctantly hopped to his feet and followed.

The Casbah was considerably different from the way it had been the night before.

German soldiers were no longer in the majority. Though the Germans were plentiful, the crooked streets were dominated by animals. Camels, cows, pigs, goats, and fowl butted against one another, cooperating more readily than the men who peddled them or the milk or eggs they produced or whatever sugar, tea, rice, cloth, and coffee they could get their hands on. Merchants barked prices at passersby, undercutting one another and often ignoring customers while they argued. The heat and odor were oppressive, though Livingston was convinced the men smelled worse than their animals.

If Colon had any impressions about the place, he was keeping them to himself. Livingston hoped that no one looked at the private cross-eyed; he wouldn't put it past him to explode, regardless of the consequences.

They paused at one of the stands in the market to purchase tools they would need to get to the prison that night. Leaving the crowded Casbah, the men stayed clear of the docks; if Delphine were there, they didn't want her to see them. Instead, they walked through a section of the city built by the French in the previous century. The architecture reminded Livingston of New Orleans. Escott had dubbed it the French Quarter, and as they passed through, Livingston was fascinated by the blend of old and new, from the Moorish Palais des Rais to the beautiful Jardin de Prague, location of an ancient Roman necropolis.

The men also kept their eyes open for transportation.

"You're the automobile expert," Livingston said after they'd spent several minutes walking through the area. "See anything you can get to work?"

For the first time since they'd met, Colon was smiling. "Yeah. Up ahead."

Livingston followed his gaze to an Afrika Korps motorcycle. The black bicycle had two mailbags on either side and, like most vehicles in Algiers, was covered with a thick layer of desert dust and mud from the beach.

It was also the only vehicle on the street that had an armed guard: There was a sentry posted right outside the government building in front of which it was parked.

"You better make another choice," Livingston said.

"No, sir. That's what we're taking. The way I figure it, if anyone tried to chase us, we'd better be in a position to give 'em a faceful of dirt."

Colon had a point. The sentry happened to look over then, and Livingston bent to tie his shoe. "How long to hotwire it?"

"Maybe half a minute."

Livingston looked down the street. Several doors away, a pair of officers were standing outside a bakery. Further down, at a café, an Arab was trying to sell ivory-handled knives to three other officers. There was no one else about.

"All right," Livingston said. "I'm game."

While Colon pretended to admire the motorcycle, Livingston went up to the sentry.

"Pardon me, but is *Oberstapotheker* von Rundstedt here?"

"I'm sorry, there is no apothecary colonel here. Only Generalmajor Mantell and his staff."

"There must be some mistake." Livingston reached into his pocket, withdrew his papers, and handed them to the sentry. The guard lay his service rifle aside. "You see here, *schutze*, I was sent to—"

The moment the guard looked at the papers, Livingston grabbed the back of the young man's neck, pushed down, and brought his own knee up. The sentry's skull cracked audibly and he slumped backward.

Livingston hurried to the street. "How's it going?"

Colon had finished stripping one of the two ignition wires. He began on the second. "I'm a little behind. These things were hidden way the hell in there."

Livingston looked back at the building. "Better hurry up, fella. Mail's here."

The mail carrier was coming down the corridor. Livingston hurried back to the building and bent over the guard just as the mailman emerged.

"What happened?" the newcomer asked.

"He passed out. Give me a hand, will you?"

As the mailman bent to help, the motorcycle engine roared. He looked over. "Hey! What are you doing?"

"Special delivery," Livingston said as he drove an uppercut into the man's belly. The mail carrier went down. "Let's go!" Livingston yelled as he ran toward the street.

The private revved the engine. It coughed and

he nursed the choke, then gently twisted the throttle. "Please, hon, don't crap out on me."

The mail carrier pulled himself to his feet. "Help! Someone *stop* them!"

Down the street, the officers outside the bakery looked over; one of them spotted the fallen guard. He started toward the motorcycle. "You there! What's going on?"

"Come *on*," Livingston urged as he hopped onto the seat behind Colon.

The engine was still sputtering when Colon shifted gears. The bike lurched ahead.

And stalled.

Livingston scrambled off the seat. "Let's get out of here. *Leave* it!"

Colon shook his head violently. He glowered at the splice beside the cam cover. "Its just the goddamn dust. I'll have it fixed in a second." He slid from the motorcycle, and looked back. Then, in a quick, fluid movement that reminded Livingston of a scene from a Western movie, he spun and shot both the officer and the mail carrier. The remaining Germans took cover in doorways.

Colon bent back over the bike. "Don't say it, Sergeant. I'm with Chadli on this: They're the goddamn enemy."

Livingston crouched behind the motorcycle and fired at the soldiers down the street. He also shot at the men who had entered the corridor of the building. While he squatted there, he thought back to something Escott had told them.

"There are two ways to go about an operation such as this: with firepower or with subtlety. With only five men on the team, you are to use the latter. Blend in with your surroundings. Be as inconspicuous as possible."

They'd blended in all right. If the city hadn't been on alert before, it would be now.

Colon blew off the stripped ends of the wires and knotted them again. The motorcycle started up, sounding healthier than before. Colon throttled up and the engine ran smoothly.

"Let's go!" he said, and as soon as Livingston swung on they tore down the street, easily outstripping the men who ventured, now, out of the building.

As the French Quarter gave way to a field of low hills spotted with almond trees, Livingston tried not to think about how they could have done this differently. With less than two days before the landings, he told himself that only one thing mattered: whether or not the mission succeeded.

With that in mind, Livingston began reviewing the things they'd been told about the enemy aerodrome.

The layout. The planes they had to hit. The numbers of soldiers there, according to intelligence reports.

Livingston found it difficult to concentrate. At the same time, being out in the open helped to make things clearer. Away from the madness of the hills, of Algiers, of the war, he savored the warm breeze, the eternal sands and mountains all around him. He found himself wondering how any ruler could dare try to impose his will, his culture, on a magnificent land such as this.

Hitler's arrogance was nearly as great as his cruelty. And while Livingston could never be like Colon, a cowboy who blasted anything that moved, the more he saw of men like Franco and Hitler, the prouder he was to be fighting them.

Now, all he had to do was find a way to beat them.

Weyers awoke with a thumping headache and the fear that he'd gone blind. Everything was dark. He spit out pieces of straw and climbed slowly to his feet.

He exhaled with relief. There was a dim square of light a few paces away; it was coming from between bars in a door. At least he could still see. He reached back, gently felt at his scalp. There was a scab and he felt a shooting pain when he touched where he'd been hit. It was probably a mild concussion, but at least the knock on the head hadn't done any permanent damage.

The pigs. He'd surrendered, but they hadn't even had the decency to treat him like a prisoner of war. Instead of taking him in at gunpoint, the lazy bastards had clubbed him. They had no class. No balls. And if he had anything to say about it, no future.

In the distance, he heard whimpering. The sharp snap of what sounded like a whip. A muffled German voice.

Weyers knew where he was and what was going on. He also knew that he had to get the hell out of there, and immediately began feeling his way around the room.

He made several circuits of the small chamber. There was no furniture, no window, and the door was a solid piece of cedar whose hinges were cased in iron.

But there was *something* he might be able to use. Something that would make a hell of a weapon.

Removing his tunic, Weyers pulled off his shirt and went to work.

Chapter Nine

The low-lying hills blocked the view of the airfield as Livingston and Colon raced toward it. Through the rippling waves of early autumn heat, however, they could see planes taking off and landing in the distance, kicking up long plumes of desert sand. As the scant aerial reconnaissance had revealed, very few of the runways had been paved. Come what may, that would work to the Allies' advantage during the invasion because it would be impossible for successive waves of aircraft to take off until the dust from previous waves had settled.

As they neared, Livingston became concerned lest their own trail of dust draw someone's attention. Very soon, word of their escapade in town would reach the base; any mechanic on a motorcycle would be the object of close scrutiny. Thus, as soon as the tops of the watchtowers at the northern perimeter came into view, the men parked the bike beneath an almond tree and continued on foot. As Livingston recalled from his briefing, the narrow stretch of scrubland was spotted with almond trees according to an ancient

Arab custom: Whenever a man married or celebrated a birthday, each of his friends planted five almond seeds. As they moved from tree to tree, briefly hiding behind each, Livingston was glad the Arabs were long-lived and polygamous.

When the pair reached the last of the hills before the airbase, they dropped to their stomachs to survey the field.

And cursed in unison.

As it turned out, the Germans also had a custom, one of which the men were unaware: Whenever they fortified an area, they destroyed any and all trees, cliffs, and structures that might provide an enemy with cover.

The trees that the reconnaissance photographs had shown were no longer there, and a high barbed-wire fence had been erected. Whether this was a natural development in the fortification of the airfield, or a result of the betrayal in the SIS ranks, Livingston had no idea. Nor did it matter. There was nowhere nearby to hide until nightfall. What was worse, they'd have to find a way to get through the fence. They trained their glasses on the field and studied it for several minutes in silence.

The two paved airstrips were on the opposite side because most of the flights went out over the desert. Most of the planes they saw were Messerschmitt BF 100Es and BF 109Fs; the 110E an antitank aircraft, the other a cannon-carrying craft with a dust filter for desert fighting. All were tan with black spots or stripes, camouflaged to resemble the desert when seen from above. The fighters were lined up beside the strip, indicative of how confident the Germans were that an air strike couldn't possible succeed: It would take just one pass by Allied planes to destroy most of the air-

craft. A row of bombers sat behind the Messer-
schmitts by the second strip. From the Death's-
Head emblem on the side, just behind the cockpit,
Livingston recognized them as Heinkels.

The sergeant turned his glasses toward the
western perimeter. There were two hangars, and
between them was a squat, white building—which
Escott had presumed was a command post—
behind which was a tall, lean air-control tower. A
trio of Dornier 17Z bombers were lined up before
the hangars, no doubt being readied for attacks
on Allied shipping in the Mediterranean. Livingston couldn't see what planes were in or behind the
hangars. Beyond the farthest of the low metal
structures, however, Livingston could see the tips
of fixed antiaircraft guns—small, slender 2-cm
Flak 30s, all of which were pointed toward the
harbor. The defenders would be able to fire an
attention-getting 480 rounds a minute with those.
Well beyond the hangar, by a far fence, were eight
massive 8.8-cm Flak 18s. Slower but more powerful than the model 30s, each of those cannons
was mounted on treads, and would certainly be
moved to protect the Messerschmitts, if needed.

Beyond the 8.8-cm guns, at the very rear of the
compound, were three barracks. Livingston could
see several men smoking or playing cards outside;
a few were sunning themselves. There were many
more trucks parked than there were soldiers,
which led him to believe that more men were inside—no doubt waiting for the Allied assault on
the aerodrome, which the traitor had told them
was imminent.

Naturally, Livingston reflected, everything they
were supposed to attack was on the other side of
the field. That wouldn't have mattered if everything else had gone as planned, if they could have

used their identity papers to walk right in. It would have been relatively simple to hide the dynamite, each man taking care of four or five of the planes after they'd been loaded with bombs for the day's run. The explosions would have had a domino effect right across the airfield. There might even have been time to get a few of the antiaircraft guns.

Now that they were wanted men, just getting the explosives to the landing strip, unseen, would be a major undertaking.

"What do you think of the nearest tower?"

Livingston looked over to where Colon pointed. The tower, some fifteen meters high, rested on four stout legs. Coils of barbed wire were strung behind the two legs that faced the desert. "Looks pretty well fortified to me. What did you have in mind?"

"Since we can't go in the front door, I was thinkin' of climbing the tower. Chances are good the sentries won't be watching each other at night, so one of us does away with the guy walking the fence, puts on his uniform, and takes his place. The other guy goes up the tower and sacks the guards, which'll leave us free to haul the dynamite up and in."

Livingston scrutinized the tower. The plan wasn't anywhere near as simple as Colon made it sound. It wouldn't be possible to climb one of the four legs and get into the observation post; there was nothing on the watchtower's walls to afford a handhold. It would be necessary to go up one leg, use the struts under the lookout to swing hand over hand to a leg on the other side of the fence, then climb down and go up the stairs.

It was a difficult maneuver that would take several minutes—nearly as long as it would take to

cut through the barbed wire. However, because
they had neither wire-cutters nor light to do the
job, and would still have to contend with the guard
spotting them from above, there wasn't much
choice. Once one man had taken the tower, the
other man could climb up by rope and go inside.
There, they hoped, they would blend in and be able
to plant the charges.

"It's either that," Colon said, "or we blow up
the four towers, run in with sticks of dynamite,
and hope that one of us gets in deep enough to
blow up the planes."

"Let's leave the kamikaze stuff to the Japs. We'll
give your first plan a try and hope to hell it
works."

The men backed down the ridge. They'd planned
to go back into the hills, fetch Chadli and their
gear, and wait near the prison until nightfall. Instead, just a few moments after they started the
motorcycle, it ran out of fuel. Colon booted the
machine.

"If that ain't a kick in the head!"

"It doesn't surprise me," Livingston said. He
dropped to his knees. "Come on. Let's dig a hole
for this stiff."

After burying the bicycle in the sands, the men
set out on foot. The trek back to the city was long
and arduous, and by the time they reached the
French Quarter they needed to rest. Just outside
the city, they went behind the brick home of an
Arab who was obviously well placed in the government: There was an official black sedan in the
short driveway and, through a window, the men
could see servants.

Colon sneaked over a wooden fence to a clothes-
line. "He won't miss these," he said, stealing native attire for himself and Livingston. Colon also

took the line itself and, for appearances, snatched a baby goat that was grazing behind a nearby shanty. Donning the clothes, the men were able to pass through the city unmolested and stop at an outdoor café for a meal. All the while, groups of soldier came and went, searching shops and even their own trucks. Livingston overheard them tell an Algerian police officer that they were looking for "Allied infiltrators."

But no one bothered the two men in Arab robes, one of whom had a small goat on his lap, and a P.38 beneath it.

Early in the afternoon, refreshed, Livingston and Colon returned the goat, bought more rope, and then headed out of the city, toward the beach. Stopping at the cliff below the prison, they found a cove and took turns napping until sundown.

Lambert knew he was in trouble when they brought the wooden bench into the room.

He'd tried to make a run for it, literally broad-jumping over the bench when the two soldiers carried it in. But Hauptmann was quick and grabbed the sleeve of his tunic. The SS officer held on until a soldier ran down the corridor and drove the butt of his rifle into Lambert's jaw. The Frenchman fell to one knee, tried to get up, and was struck again in the back. He was barely con-scious when they carried him back into the cell, tore off his shirt, and strapped him belly-up to the bench.

What followed was a blur of agony, fear, and humiliation as they whipped him until the pain was continuous. But he didn't tell them what little he knew. He was rational enough to realize that the longer he said nothing, the longer he would live. However, Lambert did allow himself to scream, almost from the moment the officer started beating him. Pride be damned, he thought after the first blow. It was one less thing he'd have to worry about. He shouted oaths at the Germans whenever they stopped long enough for him to catch his breath, and he rubbed his wrists and ankles raw trying to squirm out from under each new blow.

When they finally took their bench and left him crumpled on the floor, his chest, thighs, and arms were lacerated. The hot licks of pain refused to subside; it hurt to breathe.

The door of the cell next to his opened. He had heard them talk about the "giant enemy" they'd brought in, and figured they must somehow have captured Weyers. But the voice he heard wasn't that of one of his comrades. Lambert listened, and when the beating began and the prisoner screamed, he forced himself to his feet.

"Nazi *cochon*!" His shoulders ached from the beating, but he began pounding on the wall. "Nazi *pig*!"

No one responded—except for the prisoner, who screamed.

And screamed again.

"I am *innocent*!" Delphine Dupre hollered. "*I had nothing to do with these men!*"

The woman's cries cause Ogan to start. For the moment, he forgot about Barker. He went to the door, pressed his ear to the window. He heard Lambert shouting.

"They aren't hurting her!" Ogan yelled. "It's a trick to break us!"

Lambert stopped yelling. Ogan listened. He no longer heard the cracking of the crop. But the woman continued to scream as the officer questioned her.

Ogan began to doubt himself. He paced the cell. What if they *were* torturing her? God only knew what they could invent to torment her.

But why? She was working for the Germans. Who else *could* have been the security leak? It couldn't be one of the team members. If any of them had talked, there would be no reason to torture the others. They would all have been taken out and shot.

Escott or Sweet? The chicken farmer? Someone on the American side?

No one else knew about the operation!

Her screams seemed genuine, and his temples throbbed again. Could he save her *and* Barker by telling them what he knew? Was there some way the Nazis could guarantee their safety?

Ogan went to the door, took a deep breath to call to the SS officer. He hesitated. Could he really betray his country . . . and so many soldiers?

The woman gurgled and moaned. Then shrieked. Ogan turned from the door and flopped down. He grabbed fistfuls of hay, squeezing until they crumbled.

He gazed blindly through the dark. The hay. It had fallen apart. It was dry.

It would burn.

It was a longshot, but if he could start a fire the tinderbox prison would go up like kindling. He looked around. He could try using his belt buckle to strike a spark on the stone. Maybe he could get them to leave him alone with a cigarette.

No. He had a better idea. He leaped to his feet and ran to the door. *"Herr Oberstleutnant! Come here!"*

After a moment, the woman's moans subsided. Her cell door opened and there were footsteps in the corridor. Hauptmann looked into Ogan's cubicle.

"Yes, Sergeant Major? You wish to tell me something?"

"I want to cooperate."

From the next cell Ogan heard—much to his surprise—the voice of Jamie Weyers. "Bloody traitor!"

When was he captured? Did that mean Livingston and Colon had been taken as well? Ogan's heart raced as he realized that the entire mission might well depend on what he did next.

Anxious as he was, he felt better than he did when he'd considered capitulating.

The SS officer barked for Weyers to be silent. He called for his aide. Ogan stepped to the side of the door. All he'd need was a few seconds. Create the fire, get the soldier's gun, use the smoke to shield his actions. He held his breath while the key turned in the lock.

The door opened . . .

Arab robes are loose fitting to allow for ventilation in the desert. They're so spacious that nomads pitch small tents with them, propping the robes with a stick and sitting cross-legged beneath them.

But the robes were not meant for climbing, something Colon discovered when he tried to get a foothold nearly halfway up the sea cliff.

Because the nearly three-hundred-feet climb was too much for either man to make on his own, it had been decided that Colon would take the first half and lower the rope. Because the handholds were farther apart higher up, Livingston would take the second.

For the third time since starting his ascent, Colon had stepped on a fold in the robe. This time, however, he'd nearly yanked himself down. Reaching the ledge and tying the rope to it, he ripped off the garment, deciding that it didn't much matter whether an Arab or a German mechanic was seen scaling the cliff beneath the jail. Either way, he'd be a dead man; he might as well be a comfortable one.

Colon lowered the rope to Livingston, who, after discarding his own robe, shimmied up to Colon's side and began the second half the ascent.

Neither man had ever done any climbing, which was good. Had they known what they were getting into, they might not have tried it. Few of the rocks were more than knoblike outcroppings, none offered a firm hand or foothold, and most were slippery from the sea breeze. Toward the top, for nearly the last quarter of its height, the cliff was nearly sheer; Livingston proceeded so slowly that, at times, nearly a minute would pass before Colon heard the telltale crunch of shoes or the sound of dislodged pebbles dropping to the beach. On occasion, Livingston had to use his dagger to cut fingerholds in the rock.

At last, the end of the rope dropped next to Colon and he climbed up. He found Livingston crouched, dirty and perspiring, on the narrow shelf of rock between the cliff and the prison. As soon as both men had had a chance to catch their breath, they moved quietly along the back wall of the prison.

As they'd noticed from below, there was only one way into the prison from the back: a window that let into a small office. The shutters were thrown open, and a gentle night wind rustled the blackout curtains that had been hung inside. The men looked in.

Suddenly, gunshots rang from inside. Swearing, Livingston and Colon climbed in.

The instant the cell door opened, Ogan jumped at the soldier with the lantern. He used a judo hold to grab the man and slam him against the wall, then spun and kicked the door shut.

A moment's delay, that was all he'd need. Ogan used that instant to wrench the lantern away and shatter the globe with his foot. The flame spread quickly. But the soldier was more resilient than Ogan had anticipated, and he threw a punch; though the blow was wild, it caused Ogan to duck.

That cost him time. And it was all the time the German needed. He launched himself at Ogan just as the door swung open and the SS officer stepped in, his gun drawn. He ordered his aide back. Ogan stood there, cornered in the flickering light of the fire, as Hauptmann called for help to put out the fire.

Ogan felt a familiar weakness in his knees. His plan had backfired; the only way to save Barker now was to cooperate.

To blazes with that!

Even if he could have brought himself to cooperate with the enemy, one look at the officer told him that conciliation wouldn't save anyone. The hard set of the German's jaw, the fury in his eyes—this man intended to kill them all.

Submitting was no way for it to end and, snarling, Ogan jumped at the officer. Hauptmann's gun coughed twice and the Englishman fell.

The German's face registered surprise. He poked the man with his toe. *"Narrisch Englander! Fool!"* He stepped back from the flames. *"Where is the water?"*

"Over here, asshole!"

Hauptmann looked back just as Colon shot two men with buckets, then fired at the officer. Hauptmann fell forward into the spilled water, his blood spreading quickly across the floor.

"Now who's foolish, you Kraut bastard?"

Three soldiers had been standing at the far end of the corridor. When the shooting had erupted, one of them opened the door to the nearest cell to take cover. Colon and Livingston took cover behind a wall; no sooner had they done so than one of the soldiers came flying back into the corridor, his hands clutching his throat, blood seeping between his fingers. A second man followed, a diagonal slash across his chest. There were sounds of a struggle; after a moment the third man fell out, holding his side. Weyers stormed after him, punching the wounded man hard in the face. There was an explosion of blood and the German fell back.

"What's the matter, don't like my company?"

Moments later, a man bolted from Ogan's flaming cell firing a spray of gunfire; Colon and Livingston dove back as Weyers jumped at the man's back. The German stopped, wheezed, and rose slightly from the ground. Then the South African jerked his arm back and the man dropped limply to the ground.

Weyers looked down the hall at his teammates. He wiped another man's blood from his chin. "That's how I like my Nazis. Deader than Attila."

Livingston came down the corridor. He stole a look at the six-inch lantern hook held tightly between the third and fourth fingers of Weyers's right hand. In Weyer's hand, it was one of the most formidable-looking weapons he'd ever seen.

While Colon ran to get the keys from Weyers's cell, Livingston went to see about Ogan. The cell was filled with smoke and flame, and he called for

Weyers. Together, they lifted Ogan into the corridor. His shirt was wet with blood.

"Is he alive, Sergeant?"

Livingston didn't answer. When they reached the hallway, they lay the Englishman down and carefully undid his shirt. There was a raw, red hole in his chest and another in his side.

"Looks bad," Weyers said, looking down.

"Hey!" Colon yelled. "I need some help back here. We've got a legion of the walking dead!"

Livingston and Weyers hurried back. On the way, the American saw some of the other prisoners, men and women who were helping one another escape into the night. Many of them could barely walk; there was even a pair of children there, two boys who were pale, thin, and afraid. A woman came and quickly spirited them away.

Reaching the far side of the prison, Livingston and Weyers found Colon in a cell, helping Lambert to his feet. The private cocked his head toward the corridor.

"There are two more prisoners," he said, "both ours."

The men hurried over. In one, they found a heap that was barely human. They guessed it was Barker. Weyers gathered him in gently in his arms. In the last, Livingston found Delphine. She was naked and sobbing, crouched in a pool of dirt and dark blood.

There was no doubt in his mind that she hadn't betrayed them. Which meant that somewhere, here or at home, there was still a traitor at large.

Perhaps, he had to admit, even in the Force Five team itself.

Chapter Ten

Livingston had driven the half-track well into the hills before reinforcements arrived from the city.

Staff cars and troop transports alike descended on the burning prison. Weyers watching through glasses as men jumped from the vehicles and began pumping well water into buckets. A few men swathed themselves in wet blankets and went inside. The big South African smiled. They wouldn't be able to save the prison. By tomorrow morning, there would be one less Nazi horror chamber.

Content, he walked back to the high ledge on which Livingston had parked. There was only one way up here, a winding path easily defensible from behind the large rocks and old walls. The truck was parked well back, invisible from below.

The campsite looked like a hospital ward. Ogan lay in the open back of the vehicle; Colon sat with Delphine in the front. Lambert was sprawled on a blanket that had been spread on the ground. Not far from him lay the body of Harold Barker, his face covered with Weyers's tunic.

Working by the light of a lantern they'd taken from the prison. Livingston used antiseptic from the half-track's first aid kit to clean Ogan's wounds. He'd worked out the bullets with his knife; the surgery hadn't been clean, but it had been thorough.

"How is he?"

"Still unconscious," Livingston said, "but his breathing's steady. What's happening at the prison?"

"Soldiers from the city just got there. No one seems to have noticed our tracks. I think we'll be okay for a while."

Livingston nodded and Weyers walked over to Lambert. The Frenchman was smoking, enjoying the breeze that brushed across his naked chest and arms.

"How do you feel, Rotter?"

"Like hell."

"You *look* like hell."

"*Merci*. Now tell me something, my big, brave hero. How is it that you managed to escape a beating?"

Weyers snorted. "They knew it would be a waste of time. Besides, I was ready for them."

"Were you? How?"

Weyers pulled the hook from his pocket. He displayed it proudly. "I got four of them with this."

"The lantern hook? But how did you get it out of the brick?"

"I wound my shirt around it, put my foot against the wall, and pulled." He slipped it between his fingers. "Back in Pretoria, we used to do this with skinners, small knifes that we held in the fist." He slashed in several directions to show how it worked. "Very effective."

Lambert blew smoke from his nostrils. "I'm impressed. Back in Sousse, do you know what I learned as a child? How to grab snakes by the head before they could bit you. *Alors*, that's not very helpful now, but it used to impress the young girls."

Chuckling, Weyers climbed into the half-track. After making himself comfortable, he told Lambert about how he once strung his shoelaces across a doorway to trip up a police officer.

Colon pushed strands of blonde hair from Delphine's forehead. She looked up from the cup of water and smiled.

"I want to thank you again for all you've done, Ernesto. You're a very gentle man."

Colon wriggled uncomfortably. "I ain't done anything big. *You're* the hero. You're the one who stood up to them."

The young woman looked away, said nothing.

They were sitting in the front of the half-track, Delphine in the passenger's seat and the private on the fender, beside the extra oil can. She was wearing his tunic and her own torn dress, which he'd retrieved before they left. He'd also paused to spit on the SS officer for what they'd done to her. In her cell, an iron bar covered with blood told the story.

Colon brushed her cheek, feeling ashamed for the way the team members had doubted her. Each of them had faced death this past day, but none of them had suffered the brutal degradation Delphine had endured. What astonished him most was that she'd insisted on walking to the half-track. Every step was agony, but she'd done it. The Nazis weren't going to rob her of her dignity.

Colon had helped stop the bleeding and cleaned her. He'd wanted her to rest, but she'd asked him to stay; they sat, barely speaking, while she ate rations they found in the back of the half-track.

Colon usually felt uncomfortable around women, but not with Delphine. Though he knew nothing about her except what he saw in her eyes, the determination and strength he found there told him all he needed to know.

Ogan regained consciousness with a start.

Livingston had finished bandaging his wounds when the Englishman jumped; Weyers had to be called over to help restrain him.

"Easy," Livingston said, "you've lost a lot of blood."

"Harold! Must . . . get to . . . Harold!"

"Harold's with us. You lie still."

Panting, Ogan lay back. "Where . . . are we?"

"In the hills, about a kilometer from the prison."

"Is everyone . . . safe?"

"The whole team."

"Barker?'

Livingston looked at Weyers. He's been so busy with Ogan, he hadn't checked on the others. The South African shook his head.

"He's resting," Livingston said.

Ogan continued gasping for breath. Livingston used his index finger to loosen the bandages near Ogan's throat. "What about . . . the aerodrome?"

"Tomorrow," Livingston said. "The explosives are safe in the hills, and we should be able to do everything we were sent to do."

Ogan seemed to relax slightly. "Good. Look after Barker . . . I'll be all right."

"Sure."

Livingston patted him on the leg, then climbed down. He and Weyers shared water from a German canteen as they walked about the hilltop.

"How's your head?" Livingston asked.

"Broke, but I'll live. I'm in better shape than Ogan. What do you think his chances are?"

"Okay, as long as we don't go jostling him around. The guy really needs sutures, not bandages."

"We can leave him with Delphine."

Livingston nodded. "That's what I was thinking. We certainly can't take him with us."

"Speaking of which, it would seem as though Delphine isn't our leak. What do you think, then? Someone back in England?"

"It's possible, but unlikely. Don't forget, the Germans didn't know how many of us were coming over or where we were landing. Anyone involved in the Force Five project back home knew that information."

"True. Which leaves who?"

"I'm not sure." Livingston had his own suspicions, but before he said anything that might prejudice the men, he wanted to make certain. "Listen, I'm going to get Chadli and do a little more reconnoitering. Think you can hold down the fort until morning?"

"I hate like hell sitting around like this. I'd rather go with you."

"Thanks, but Colon's a little preoccupied, and I don't want to leave him alone."

"I figured you'd say that." Weyers looked back, past the half-track. "I guess it'd be smarter if I found someplace around here to leave Ogan and the girl."

"And Lambert."

Weyers snorted. "Forget it, mate. He may have to crawl, but there's no way he'll pass up a good scrap. Especially if Jerry's involved. He's got balls that clang, that one."

"All right. We'll meet on the south hill, Chadli's

farm, at dawn. That'll give us time to go over the plan, dispense the explosives, and get a little shut-eye."

They'd gone back to the half-track, and Livingston took a shovel from the equipment locker.

"What're you going to do with that?" Weyers asked.

"A little prospecting."

The South African seemed puzzled. "Well, good luck. And be careful, Sergeant. At the rate we're going, about the only thing we'll be able to do to those bombers is bleed on them."

Livingston smiled, and after the men shook hands he set off into the hills to see if his suspicions were correct. To see if what he'd seen at the prison was accurate.

To see if someone hadn't been practicing a grand deception on them.

The hill reminded him of something from *The Bride of Frankenstein*: a graveyard consisting of long mounds of dirt, unevenly spaced, with cold stones and a dark, cloudy sky above.

None of the mounds was marked, but that didn't matter. Livingston saw the ones he was looking for. Short ones. Four graves in which children would have been buried.

He put his foot to the shovel, tried not to think about what he was doing. He didn't believe in an afterlife, and he didn't believe that any kind of god was going to punish him. But that didn't soften the grisly nature of the enterprise.

The dry earth came up easily, and in less than a minute he'd uncovered the first grave: that of a girl, her small body stitched with black holes from a machine gun. Livingston looked away. He breathed through his mouth to keep from vomiting as he buried her and went to the second of the four small mounds. There was another girl here, younger than the first. He covered the hole and went to the third grave. This one was empty. So was the fourth. And Livingston knew that if he uncovered the rest of the graves, one of those belonging to an adult would also be empty.

The grave of a woman with beautiful green eyes. A grave dug so that no one who worked with the Allies would be the wiser.

The grave of Chadli's wife.

Leaving the cemetery, Livingston moved through the hills with the speed and stealth of a predator. His footsteps were light and quick; even his breathing was shallow and soundless. He couldn't afford to be heard. He had to be the one who found his prey, and not the other way around.

As he passed the farm where the partisans had been executed, Livingston didn't know how he felt. It was clear that Chadli had lied about his family, that he'd agreed to help the Nazis if they would spare his wife and sons. Livingston had seen them at the prison; they were wan but alive, the only prisoners who didn't show some signs of having been beaten. No doubt Chadli was allowed to visit them regularly, to make certain they were all right.

Ironically, Chadli had seized the opportunity to butcher the soldier in the hills because he knew he could get away with it. Chadli obviously detested the Germans nearly as much as he loved his family.

But he'd also betrayed Barker and the Force Five team. And if Livingston wasn't mistaken, the Algerian had one more deception up his sleeve. A trick that, even now, might be too late to prevent.

Weyers found a hut some four hundred meters along the cliff, one with a cellar concealed by a straw mat. Judging from the broken hookahs and hashish pipes, drug smugglers had worked here, watching the harbor for their ships; presumably, they'd given up their trade when the Mediterranean became too crowded with warships. From what he'd heard, the amount of drug trafficking down by the Nazis themselves was enough to put even the most ambitious smuggler out of business.

But the hut still stood, and the cellar was long and dark enough so that only a thorough investigation would find anyone inside. He didn't think the Germans would waste the time or risk losing soldiers in such a search.

Colon and Weyers carried Ogan over on a stretcher they'd made from the canvas top of the half-track. When they put him down behind a row of empty crates, he awoke and tried to climb off. Weyers gently pushed him back down; Ogan was stronger and more alert then he expected.

"Easy, Sergeant. You move and you'll start bleeding like a bloody faucet."

"Never mind . . . me. The mission—"

"It's going fine. Colon, Lambert, and I are going to rendezvous with Livingston. You'll stay here with Delphine."

"No!" He started to get up again. "I . . . won't stay behind!"

Weyers pressed him back more firmly and Ogan grabbed the front of his shirt; the South African wrested his fingers away. "I'm afraid you don't have much of a choice. Even if you *could* walk, you'd only hold us back. We can't afford to watch you every step of the way."

When the words had sunk in, Ogan sighed bitterly and shut his eyes. Weyers stepped away, relieved that he hadn't asked about Barker. They'd buried him beneath a pile of rocks shortly after Livingston had left; the South African had a feeling that when Ogan found out, his reaction would make the strange display at the warehouse seem tame by comparison.

Colon had gone back upstairs and was helping Delphine down the rope ladder. Though she still limped, she'd made an extraordinary recovery. Hate, he knew from experience, was the best medicine know to man.

The private left her his and Lambert's pistols, along with a dozen ammunition clips. He set the lantern on a crate. "Make me a promise?"

She looked at him questioningly and he folded a key into her hand.

"Tomorrow night, try to get upstairs and listen. If you don't hear us blowing the airfield to hell, promise me you'll take the half-track and. head west. The army shouldn't have any trouble taking Casablanca, and you'll be safe there."

"But why must I leave? The invasion—"

"If we fail here, chances are good the invasion will fail too."

She took his hands in hers. "I'll listen for the explosions, and when I hear them I'll sit on a crate and wait for you."

"Sure, but if there aren't any—"

"There *will* be. I believe in justice. I believe that you *will* succeed. We will celebrate in Casablanca *together*."

Colon took a quick look behind him. Weyers had gone back up to the hut. Taking the woman in his arms, he hugged her tightly. "You're a brick."

"And you are *mon soldat heroique*. Good luck,"
she said into his ear, and clutched him closer.

Generalmajor Mantell was a soft man with a
hard face, a man who had enjoyed the good life in
Berlin before being assigned to Algiers.

He didn't like this city. He didn't like the heat,
the smell, the people, the animals, the lack of culture. He didn't like the sewage that ran down the
streets, and he didn't like the wine or food.

But the thought of losing Algiers for Hitler was
something he liked even less, and as soon as he
learned of the attack he had gone directly to the
prison.

Antiaircraft batteries along the shore were put
on alert. Fighters had been scrambled. This might
be the prelude to the invasion that had been ru-
mored for months. Mantell hoped so. With nothing more to do here than find, interrogate, and
execute partisans, his men were getting stale—as
this disaster had demonstrated.

Before any of the surviving prison staff had been
allowed to go to the hospital, Mantell had questioned them personally. They all said the same
thing about the commandos.

"Well organized . . . nine or ten of them . . . machine guns."

He doubted that. There were only two sets of
footprints below the cliff, by the rope the commandos had used. The late Hauptmann was a good
warden, but his forte was brutality, not soldiering. He and his SS people would say anything to
justify failure.

Regardless of how many men there were, or how
well armed they might be, the enemy was *not* failing. However many men there were, they were a

brave and efficient unit and they had to be stopped.

After returning to headquarters, the major general sat in his office and tried to reach a decision. The double agent had told them that the aerodrome was the target of the commandos. That made sense, and Mantell had already ordered two regiments shifted from the makeshift barracks at the harbor to the aerodrome. But he wondered if it was worth keeping his troops on alert for that attack while the commandos struck throughout the city. Instead of a few companies poking through the hills, perhaps the time had come to take the fight to them in earnest, to send a battalion or two to flush them out.

It was a dangerous maneuver; there would be chaos if an attack on the aerodrome came *now* and he had to start calling men in from the field. But the commandos had to be stopped and, hoping to boost morale by hanging these men in public, he picked up the phone and asked to be connected with the base commander.

Chapter Eleven

The men marched single file.

Leading the group was Weyers, whose huge bulk looked more bearlike than ever with blood splattered on his hands, arms, face, and clothing. Behind him, Lambert's bare chest was crisscrossed with blood, and he grimaced whenever a move opened a wound or foliage scraped at him. Colon brought up the rear. His determination to wreak havoc was underscored by the pistol in his holster, the pistol tucked in his belt, and the knife held tight in his right hand. Yet his expression was the most formidable element of all. From his dark eyes to his rigid jaw, his face was a mask of grim purpose.

The men spotted Livingston easily as they neared the glen where Chadli's barn had stood. Though dawn had arrived, Livingston had made no effort to conceal himself. He was seated behind a boulder on the top of the northern hill. Beside him were the two meal sacks of explosives.

He turned almost casually as the men approached. There was an uncharacteristically glum expression on his face.

"What's wrong?" Weyers asked.

Livingston reached into one of the canvas bags and pulled out a stick of dynamite. "Hold this," he said.

Weyers did as he was told. Fishing out a carton of matches, Livingston lit the fuse. It hissed, throwing a pale yellow light across Weyers's startled eyes.

"Jesus! What are you doing?"

"Just hold on to it," Livingston said, and sat back against the rock.

The other men stood back from Weyers. He looked from Livingston to the dynamite. "You wouldn't happen to be the traitor in our group," the South African said uneasily as he watched the fuse shrink. "If you are, just remember that this'll also blow you to—"

There was a hollow pop, followed by a spray of gray green powder. The men stared aghast at the shattered cylinder in Weyers's hand.

"Blow me to where?" Livingston asked. "The dynamite's packed with talc. Chadli's the son of a bitch who's been screwing us. The Krauts didn't kill his family. They took them prisoner. As long as Chadli cooperated, his wife and kids were kept alive."

Weyers swore. Lambert whistled. Colon squeezed the knife handle.

Livingston pointed to the sacks of explosives. "I cut into every damn stick, hoping just one of them would be live. Nothing."

Weyers sat down heavily. "So even if we got in, we couldn't have blown up a balloon. And it would have been too late to do a damn thing about it."

Livingston nodded. "The crazy thing is, you know what frost me the most? We're the ones who let the guy's wife and kids out."

"When?" Weyers scratched his bald head.

"I saw them at the prison, recognized the wife from Chadli's description. That's what tipped me off." He sighed heavily. "By now the four of them are probably halfway to Morocco. We can't even wring the little rat's neck."

The men were silent for a long moment. Lambert finally spoke up. "We're not going to abandon the mission, are we? There's got to be *something* we can do."

"I'm going in there, even if I have to take the planes apart with a screwdriver," Weyers said.

"Assuming we can even get one," Livingston said bitterly. "I have a feeling that after last night, the enemy won't be taking us for granted anymore."

"Suppose we *could* get inside," Colon said. "How would we destroy the planes?"

"Getting inside is a pretty big thing to suppose," Lambert pointed out.

"Maybe not. The question is, could any of us do enough damage to make a difference?"

"You were there," Weyers said. "What did the field look like?"

"It's a big sandbox with a high barbed-wire fence and four observation towers," Livingston answered. He picked up a stick and sketched a picture in the soil. He indicated where the airstrips, hangars, and airplanes were located.

Weyers studied the map intently, then rubbed it out with his foot. "Y'know, one of the things that hurt your boys at Pearl Harbor was the way the planes were bunched together on the runway. The Japs just swooped in and blew the hell out of them. From the look of it, the aerodrome is laid out pretty much the same. There isn't a hell of a lot of solid ground out there, and only two strips are paved, so they've got to make the best of what space they have."

"Meaning?"

"One bomber, flying low, could do an awful lot of damage."

Lambert threw up his hands. "*Bien!*" he gasped, wincing from the pain. "All we have to do . . . is get our hands on a bomber."

"There're at least a half dozen of them at the field," Weyers said.

Livingston's mood changed abruptly. "Weyers, do you think you could *fly* one of their planes?"

"I've done it before. There're very few aircraft that I couldn't figure out how to get off the ground."

"So we've decided to steal a German plane," Lambert said. "Fine, but I still want to know how we're going to get *into* the damn aerodrome!"

"I can do it," Colon said.

"Colon," Livingston said, "if you're still thinking about climbing one of the towers, forget it. My guess is they'll have doubled the guards after what we did at the prison."

"Probably. But that'll work to our advantage."

"How?"

Colon proceeded to explain his plan. When he was finished, Lambert let out a small cheer.

"If I owned a hat, I would hurl it into the air. The idea is *magnifique!*"

After mulling it over, Livingston agreed. If nothing else, it was something no one in their right mind would try; the element of surprise, if not downright confusion, would certainly be in their favor.

The air was as stale as any Ogan could ever remember tasting, and in his many years of service, working in prisons and pulling bodies from bombed-out buildings in Coventry, he'd breathed some foul air.

The room—if it was a room—was stuffy and rank, fouled even more by his own odor, the stench of blood and sweat.

It was worse than Coventry—but where was he? Slowly, he opened his eyes. It was pitch black, save for an orange glow that came from somewhere around a corner. He went to sit up—and suddenly, it was no longer black. White light flashed everywhere, the glow of pain. Moaning, he fell back.

Ogan heard footsteps, but his eyes were shut so tightly he couldn't open them to see who was coming. He heard a voice, a sweet French voice, and listened to it as the pain began to subside.

"Monsieur Ogan, you mustn't move."

The voice was familiar. He tried to place it. "Why—what happened?"

"You were shot . . . at the prison. Livingston took care of you."

He relaxed as the white light faded. "God, I don't remember anything."

"I'm not surprised. Between the shooting and our escape, you've been through a great deal."

The voice. It couldn't be. Slowly, Ogan opened his eyes. Even in the dim light of the lantern, he recognized the blonde hair and pale blue eyes.

"Delphine?"

"Yes. Now rest . . ."

Ogan's brow wrinkled. Was this a trap? Were the Germans trying to make him believe that they were free? Were they using Delphine to find out what he knew of the invasion.

"The prison," he said. "What happened there?"

"Don't worry about that now. We're safe, and you must not—"

"No!" He tried to sit again but fell back. "The others! What happened? Where ... where *are* they?"

She quieted Ogan and told him; as she did so, fragments of memory returned. He recalled the fire. The SS officer shooting at him. Lying outside somewhere with Livingston next to him, trying to talk.

"Barker!" Ogan climbed onto an elbow, this time ignoring the pain. "What happened to him?" Delphine tried to push him back, but he resisted. "*My friend Barker*. Where *is* he?"

Delphine was exasperated. "Do you mean the other man we took from the prison?"

Ogan nodded.

"I'm sorry to say, he is dead. They buried—"

Ogan's scream took her by surprise. She recoiled and he pushed her aside. He rose slowly, leaning against the wall for support.

"*Monsieur!* What are you *doing*?"

The Englishman didn't answer. He stumbled down the narrow corridor, gasping from pain but never stopping. As he groped through the dark, Delphine grabbed the lantern and ran after him. "Where are you going? If you go out, they may see you!"

"I don't care."

"You *must*! Here, at least, we can defend ourselves!"

Sobbing and hacking, Ogan reached the rope ladder. He hooked an arm through the top rung and groaned, his chest on fire.

"This is *madness*! You can no longer *help* him!"

Ogan dragged himself up. He hung there, the

rung in the crook of his arm, as he pushed at the mat.

Barker was dead. *Murdered.* A good man had died, needlessly, and at the hands of those who hated him. He'd deserved more. At the very least, Barker deserved the kind of friend he himself had been—one who would have done something to help him when he had the chance. Ogan remembered everything now, all too vividly. Instead of helping, he'd tried a lunatic scheme to escape. *What had he been thinking?*

The mat fell into the cellar and daylight filled the hole. Delphine reached for him and tried to restrain him. Ogan was crying openly as he wrenched himself from her hands.

"Monsieur, *please!"*

"Get away! My friend died alone. I won't leave him *now."*

Ogan slipped down a rung as pain stabbed through him. Breathing deeply, he forced himself back up to the hole. Reaching through, he clawed at the ground until he was out of the cellar.

Delphine followed. "If you must do this, at least let me help you!" Bending beside him, she held Ogan around the waist, lifting him to relieve the strain on his chest. His arm dropped around her shoulders and they hobbled from the hut toward the stones that made up the simple grave.

The plan required an Algerian, and though Lambert could pass as a native, he needed the proper attire. Getting it proved easy, if distasteful.

Because they didn't dare return to the city, and couldn't count on the cooperation of any of the farmers who lived in the hills, Livingston took the men to Chadli's cemetery. There, they looked in all of the graves until they found a man whose clothing would fit Lambert.

They told themselves the dead Resistance fighter would have approved of this chance to strike out at the enemy from beyond the grave. But that didn't make the chore any more pleasant.

The odor was awful, but the Frenchman was pragmatic. "At least now I *smell* like a native as well," he said as he slipped on the robe.

While Lambert dressed, Weyers and Colon went off to shoot and cook a rabbit. Because it was nearly noon, they had decided to wait before heading to the aerodrome. They had several kilometers of plain to cross on foot, and didn't relish doing it when the sun was directly overhead. It would drain them, and they'd need all their strength for the night ahead.

After the men ate they rested, though no one slept much. When they weren't thinking about the mission, they were holding their breath and listening to the sound of German trucks. Although the men were well hidden in the grasses high above the road, convoys passed below regularly.

"Evidently," Livingston said, "the patrols are concentrating on the roads which lead to the aerodrome and away from the prison. The Germans must figure that only fools would go through the wilderness and approach from the rear."

There was an uncomfortable silence that ended only when Lambert pointed out that T.E. Lawrence had crossed the sprawling Nefudh Desert in the last war to stage a successful attack on the city of Akaba. Livingston didn't bother to mention that Lawrence had a much larger force and was traveling on camels and not on foot. He also said nothing about the fact that a motorcycle—which was a key to their plan—was the vehicle on which Lawrence of Arabia had died.

The men set out late in the afternoon, staying in the hills and moving with extreme caution as they neared the French Quarter, the fringes of which were a mass of shanties, wells, and small gardens that lay between the hills and the fields they needed to cross. Algerians gathered to swap goods and gossip; only rarely were there any soldiers. Anywhere the suppressed natives collected, or anywhere they could move freely—such as the hills and deserts—were places the Germans tended to avoid.

Still wearing their mechanics' uniforms, Livingston and the others moved quickly through the area, Lambert gesturing grandly as though giving them a tour. No one bothered them, and they were soon headed toward the shadow of the towering crags of Djebel Ouarsenis.

Delphine heard it first.

Ogan was kneeling beside the grave, his eyes shut, hands folded on his legs. In the few minutes that they'd been there, however, her eyes had never stopped moving, and her head turned at every sound. When she heard the sound in the distance, she wasted no time taking Ogan by the arm.

"Someone's coming."

He didn't move, and seemed completely unaware of her presence.

"Please, we must get back to the cellar!"

"I wasn't there for him," Ogan muttered. "I'll not leave him now."

The sounds grew louder. It was ironic, thought Delphine. Weyers had checked to make sure that nothing would be visible to anyone coming up this way. Not the hut, the half-track, or even the grave.

But odors—they hadn't thought of that. And the sound coming from down the hill was the barking of dogs. Behind it, she now heard the sound of an engine.

They couldn't escape using the half-track. Anything on wheels could outrun that big vehicle's treads. Worse, even if Ogan came with her now, Delphine wasn't sure there was enough time to get him back inside. If the Germans found them, they would have to fight.

Limping back to the hut, she retrieved the pistol and hid behind the half-track. She would have a clear shot at anyone who approached; if it were only a squad, and the soldiers showed themselves at once, they had a chance.

She regarded Ogan and said under her breath, "If you want to sit there, my morose friend, do so. But you're *going* to help me—as bait."

She felt her heart climb in her throat as the sounds came closer. The dogs had picked up their scent and left the road. Delphine's eyes stung from lack of sleep, but she was alert. In a way, she was even looking forward to this. Ever since the other Resistance fighters had been gunned down, she had been biding her time, waiting for a chance to strike back at the Germans. Come what may, this was an opportunity to avenge their deaths personally.

Two bloodhounds charged over a rise. Without missing a step, they ran straight for Ogan. He looked up, saw the animals, and started to rise slowly. With nothing else to support him, he wavered and fell back down.

Delphine had no idea how far away the soldiers were, or how many there were. But that no longer mattered. Steadying her right hand with her left, she fired at the dogs. The impact of the bullets blew both of them back nearly a full meter.

Delphine left the half-track and hobbled toward Ogan, who was trying to get up again. The inside of her thighs burned where the officer had violated her, but she wouldn't let the Germans take them again. She'd use a bullet on herself and one on Ogan before she allowed that to happen.

She stooped to help the Englishman, whose expression was still forlorn. He was pale, his eyes sad and wounded; under other circumstances, her heart would have gone out to him.

"Get up!"

Delphine pulled at him and he rose unsteadily. He clutched at the wound in his side; the pain caused him to suck air through his teeth. He stood still while the sounds of shouting rose from over the hill.

"Come *on*! You've got to *move*!"

Ogan put his arm around her and they started forward. He was still in a daze; Delphine knew that whoever it was in that grave, part of the Englishman was in there with him.

There was no longer a question about heading to the hut. Even if there had been time, the Germans knew that someone was up here. The cellar was a dead end. Reaching the half-track, she helped Ogan into the seat and went around to the other side just as the patrol came over the hill.

"Start the motor!" she yelled, then hobbled back and ducked behind the treads.

Ogan seemed confused. He looked at the ignition. Outside the window he saw men lying and crouching and firing on the rise.

Not his men. Germans. Nearly a dozen of them. They were firing at the truck.

"Start it, damn you!"

It was Delphine. He looked in the side mirror, saw her return their fire and pick off two soldiers before they could take cover. The others ducked behind trees and rocks. There was a pause that seemed to last an eternity.

Dear God, Ogan thought, *what have I been doing?*

Letting down Force Five and this freedom fighter, he told himself. Attending to the dead while the living needed him.

No more!

Though it hurt to move, Ogan struggled toward the wheel. Bullets pinged off the door and someone pointed at him. The Englishman slumped in the seat as a volley of shots crashed into the dashboard. Sitting low in the seat, he painfully inched his way toward the ignition key. Glass shattered, but the vehicle was parked with its back toward the men and they were unable to hit the front tires.

Reaching the driver's side, Ogan poked his head out the window. The troops proceeded in leapfrog fashion, a row of men shooting while the others advanced. He watched as Delphine returned their fire with uncanny accuracy, shooting two more men as they approached. However, that failed to deter the others. Like the guards at the prison, these men were SS, not the regulars of the Whermacht. Nothing short of a bullet through the heart would stop them. And then, not immediately.

Ogan started the engine. It turned over at once and he leaned out to see how Delphine was faring—just as a soldier got wide enough of the half-track to fire several rounds. One of his bullets hit the woman, shattering her right foot. She fell to her side, but managed to squeeze off two shots.

The soldier's forehead disappeared in a cloud of blood.

"Delphine!" Ogan threw the door open and she began clawing toward it. He tried to climb down, grew dizzy, and had to sit back. He gazed down at her, his head swimming; he'd never felt so helpless in his life, would have given anything for a gun to be able to cover her. He saw the other soldiers fan out. "Hurry!" he wheezed.

The woman's retreat was abruptly cut off by a storm of bullets. Ogan watched with horror as she spilled forward, landing on her chest, streams of blood pouring from under her body; her eyes stared up at him, lifeless.

The Germans continued to spread out, firing at the half-track. Ogan withdrew. There was nothing he could do for Delphine, but there *was* something he could do for her memory . . . and for that of Barker.

Leaning into the gearshift, he pushed the half-track in reverse; blood from the wounds wet his side. The vehicle lurched backward, the treads spitting up sand and dirt as he gunned the engine. There were shouts as the three-ton machine pressed one man into the ground and clipped another; Ogan lay to the right so he'd be below the windshield and the iron chassis would protect him from the soldiers' bullets. The half-track thumped as it rolled over one of the men Delphine had shot, then sloped back as he cleared the rise.

The men came after him and Ogan backed into a tree. He had to shift gears, losing valuable seconds as they closed in.

Suddenly, shots cracked from behind him. The Germans stopped advancing as someone opened fire on them. Two men fell; the others dropped back over the rise.

Someone came to the door of the driver's side, a short Algerian with dark skin and discolored teeth. "I've been watching from cover," he said, "but I can merely watch no longer. I owe all of you a debt which must be repaid."

Ogan wasn't able to speak, but his brow wrinkled with confusion as he slumped farther to the passenger's side. The little man climbed in.

"You must be Ogan," he said, laying the MP38 on the seat and turning the half-track around. "My name is Chadli, and I am the man who betrayed you."

Chapter Twelve

Cold and exhausted, Ogan wanted desperately to sleep. But the grinding of the treads was deafening, and with every lurch of the half-track a fresh flash of pain jolted his chest. He was thankful, at least, that his savior had stopped the bleeding. It would have been a pointless way to die, spilling out his life on the front seat of the half-track.

My savior? he thought. Was it a savior or was it Judas sitting beside him? So much of what Chadli had said Ogan found confusing. Yet the Algerian seemed to want to help him. Before coming to his aid, Chadli had put sand in the tank of the German car, making it impossible for the enemy to follow. When they had traveled several kilometers, he'd stopped to look after the Englishman's wounds. Tearing off the bottom of his robe to bind them, he'd continued on, eastward into the hills.

And then he'd talked; frankly, quickly, his voice and manner oddly joyful.

"The Nazis were holding my family," the Algerian explained. "I had no choice but to cooperate. Then, last night, I saw my loved ones at the ruins of the farm and they told me what happened. As rapidly as I could, I left them with my wife's sister and went back to the farm to try and find Livingston. There are things ... things which he needs to know about the explosives."

The ruins of the farm? Livingston had met with him? And what did he mean by "things?"

There was a great deal Ogan didn't understand, but he was too weak to ask—physically, mentally, and emotionally. Ogan was still numb when he thought of Barker in a grave, and he knew he would never feel otherwise. But what had happened to Delphine was beyond anything he'd ever experienced. He'd seen courage before, and self-sacrifices, but never to that extent.

Sometime in the afternoon, Chadli stopped by a hut. Ogan was dimly aware of him greeting a woman and children, asking for food. Foul water was poured between his own lips, along with gruel of some kind. The last thing he heard was Chadli refusing to tell the woman where he was going.

Now that the treads were silent and the half-track was still, Ogan shut his eyes and slept. He refreshed himself for what he hoped would be his turn to equal his comrades' bravery.

The sun was already dropping, and the foothills chilled quickly. Yet, as uncomfortable as the four men were, the cold didn't preoccupy them. The mission did.

After nearly three hours they reached a small lake where they rested briefly; an hour later they came to where they'd buried the motorcycle. They dug it up and Colon unfastened the leather clasps of the mailbag. He handed it to the robed Lambert, who slung it over his shoulder.

"What do you think?" the Frenchman asked. "Will I start a fashion trend in Paris?"

"Only in the circus," Weyers averred.

"You sure you've got the cover story straight?" Livingston said.

"I took the sack from the wreckage of the motorcycle. There were two bodies nearby, both of them German mechanics."

"Right. Let's hope if they think we're dead, they won't send more than two soldiers to investigate."

After shaking the hands of his comrades, Lambert set out across the rugged terrain. When he was gone, Weyers began twisting portions of the bicycle out of shape.

Lambert's feet ached. He was wearing sandals that were not only too small, but also had several holes in the heels. The mountain fighter who had worn them had also worn them out. Their condition, plus the ten kilometers he'd walked today, put him in a foul humor. If he couldn't lure two guards into the field, he vowed to kill them where they stood and take his chances against a regiment.

There were two sentries walking in opposite directions along each of the nearly quarter-kilometer-long fences. As Lambert neared the rear fence, both guards turned their rifles on him.

"Halt! Identify yourself!"

Lambert stopped and, smiling, raised his hands. "I am Omar Kabylie. I found this, sirs, and thought there might be a reward." He cocked his head toward the mail sacks. "There are letters inside. German letters. Maybe even some for you, eh?"

The soldiers looked at each other, then one of them motioned Lambert over. The other lowered his rifle but remained alert.

The young man examined the contents of the bag. "Where did you find this?"

"In the field."

"Was anything else there?"

"Yes."

The soldier looked up expectantly. Lambert smiled broadly.

"*Pasha*, I am but a poor rug merchant. I went out of my way to come here, hoping that whatever information would—"

The soldier grabbed the front of Lambert's robe. "Don't haggle with me, you filthy thing! What *else* did you see there?"

Lambert's knife was strapped to his thigh. It took all the Frenchman's self-control not to draw it. "A motorcycle, sir. And two men," he said timorously.

The German's eyes showed interest. "Two? Were they mechanics?"

Lambert held his hands palms up. "I cannot tell you what they were, sir, only what they are. And that is . . . dead."

The German held Lambert more tightly. "You killed them, didn't you? To get a reward for this!" He slapped the bags with disdain.

"No, *moulay*. I swear on my mother's good eye they were dead already! There was an accident with the motorcycle, it was twisted and—"

"I don't believe you! All Arabs are lying filth."

"Not *this* Arab!" Lambert raised his arms, as though swearing to Allah. "I am filth who speaks the truth!"

It tore at Lambert to be so fawning. But if it netted them a pair of Nazis, it was worth it.

The sentry gazed out into the field. "How far is it?"

"Only a few hundred meters."

"Show me."

The sentry poked Lambert with the barrel of his Karabiner 98k.

"Shall I come with you, Hans?" the other sentry asked.

"You are more than welcome," Lambert said quickly. It was important to get the other uniform, and this would be the easiest way to do it.

"No," Hans said, "I can handle one pig by myself." He poked Lambert again with the rifle. "Mind you, filth, I'm an expert with this. Try anything and I will shoot you."

Lambert bowed, trying not to show the annoyance he felt because the other sentry wasn't coming. "I want only to please you and win your favor."

Hans took the mailbags and handed them to the other man; with another prod from the rifle, he and Lambert set off.

The sands and scrub were a vivid orange by the time the men reached the foot of the low hill atop which the front of the broken motorcycle lay. A hand was draped over the bent fender.

"You see?" Lambert said eagerly. "I spoke the truth."

The sentry hurried ahead. Lambert came along more slowly.

Livingston could see the tension in Colon's dead body.

The private lay across the motorcycle, his arms thrown over the broken metal, his head turned back, toward his teammates. Yet even in repose, his body was a coil. Livingston hoped the German wouldn't notice that none of the limbs was askew, and that despite the blood—courtesy of the rabbit they'd had for lunch—there were no wounds.

A little farther down the incline, Weyers lay convincingly dead beside an almond tree. One hand flopped outward, another was bent under the wrist; one foot pointed up, another was folded under his ankle. His face stared toward the darkening sky, his mouth wide open. A half hour before, when both men had taken their positions, Livingston concluded that Weyers would make a hell of a bluffer in poker. Colon, on the other hand, would lose a fortune.

As had been arranged, Lambert began talking as he approached.

"You see," he said, "there is no sign of mischief. I could have taken their lovely boots, or their blouses. But you see, *wahid*, I came straight to you."

Crouched behind a rock, Livingston showed none of the disappointment he felt when he heard the word *wahid*.

If there had been two soldiers, Lambert would have called the German *itsnayn*.

Lambert stopped several paces from the motorcycle and waited while the German used the barrel of his rifle to roll Colon onto his back.

Colon suddenly reached around and grabbed the weapon. Simultaneously, Lambert threw himself at the man's legs, tackling him. Weyers wasn't needed for just one soldier, but he jumped up anyway and knelt on the mans' chest.

Furious, Lambert picked up the rifle and repeatedly jabbed the barrel into the man's shoulders and sides. "So, how do you like it? *Move*, filth! Do *this*, dirty Arab! Do *that*, disgusting pig! Where did you learn your manners, arrogant *ringa*? In a rathole?"

The German spat at him. *"Hund!"*

"And *still* you do it!" He forced the rifle barrel

between the man's lips. The German's eyes went wide. "You kiss *this*, *hund*! And if I like how you do it, maybe I won't spread your brains across—"

Livingston stepped over and pulled the gun away. "Stop this. *Now!*"

"Hey, what are you doing! You don't know the things this barbarian called me—"

"And I don't care. We need a uniform, not an apology."

"I want both!"

"Then come back and get it later!"

Lambert thrust his chin at Livingston; Weyers came over and put his hands on his friend's shoulders. "The sergeant's right, you know. Let it go, for now."

Lambert was shaking with anger. "Let so many insults go?" He tore open the front of his robe. *"They* didn't let *me* go."

"And did they get what they wanted from you? No. Pay them back by accomplishing what we set out to—"

The prisoner suddenly shrieked, and as the men looked down they saw Colon withdrawing a blade from behind the German's left ear.

"So much for *this* argument," the private said.

Livingston stared aghast at the blood oozing from the body in a thick stream.

Colon rose. "You were gonna let him live, weren't you? You were gonna tie the Kraut up and leave him until later."

"He was a prisoner of war," Livingston said.

"Yeah? And what stockade were you gonna keep him in? At least we know for *sure* that our rear is secure—and we can also stop wastin' time discussin' the dumb bastard's etiquette." The private began pulling off his own clothes. "Now are you gonna undress him, or do you want to wait 'til he bleeds all over the goddamn uniform?"

Lambert bent beside the corpse, began undoing the tunic. "He'd have done it to me."

Weyers worked on the trousers. Livingston bent and untied the shoes. The sergeant tried to take his own advice and let it go, look beyond what Colon had done and concentrate on the mission. He had no other choice.

The fit of the uniform was loose, but in the dark no one would notice that Colon wasn't the German. While the others dressed the soldier in Colon's clothes, the private lit a match and studied the dead man's identity papers.

"Hans von Varest," he muttered. "The guy deserved to die just for havin' a hoity-toity 'von' in his name."

When they were finished, Colon asked for the rifle. Livingston hesitated, and Colon leaned impatiently on one leg.

"You got somethin' on your mind, Sergeant?"

Livingston handed the Karabiner to Colon. "No. But I *would* like to know how you intend to handle the other sentry."

"We can't just call him over," Lambert said. If he becomes alarmed, he may ask the tower for a spotlight."

"Agreed. And we can't just cut his throat, either."

Weyers raised his hand. "I have an idea. We have to make him leave his post in such a way that he suspects nothing unusual, right? Dragging the motorcycle over should do it. Lambert can call for help and the sentry will see Colon struggling. He'll think it's his friend and come over. When he does, he's ours. And so is his uniform."

Lambert closed his robe as a chill wind gusted

from the mountain. He looked at Livingston. "It sounds good to me. Then Weyers and Colon can go in as soldiers, you go in as a prisoner, and I go in to collect a reward. We all go right to the planes. The only thing we have to decide before-hand is whether we're going to cut the sentry's throat or try to rehabilitate him."

Livingston regarded him sharply. "I'll take care of the sentry." He faced the others. "It's as good a plan as any. Let's move out."

Livingston crept to the edge of the low hill from which he'd first reconnoitered the aerodrome. He put the binoculars to his eyes and, after a moment, he swore.

"What is it?" Lambert asked. The Frenchman was lying behind him; the others were standing several meters back.

"There are two sentries now. The guards must have been changed."

"*Merd!*"

"You're not kidding," Livingston said. Sliding back down the hill, he informed the others. "We've got a choice. Either we risk Weyers and me both going in as Colon's prisoners, or we think of some-thing else."

"One guard going in with two POWs and an Arab?" Weyers said. "They'll never let us past the gate without an additional escort."

"And if we kill both sentries, someone may no-tice in the tower," Lambert said.

"What if we only lure one out?" Weyers asked. "Maybe the other guard'll stay put."

"That seems like our best bet," Livingston agreed, and lay below the ridge while Lambert dragged the motorcycle up the hill. Weyers walked with his hands raised, Colon holding the rifle to his back. When they reached the top, Colon called out.

"*Mein freunde!* Will one of you come and help us?"

Both sentries looked down from behind the sights of their rifles. One of them finally put aside his weapon and grabbed a flashlight.

"Who is it?"

"It's Hans," Colon barked, doing a fair impression of the man's voice. "I found the mail bicycle that was stolen, and also the man who took it. I can use a hand."

Both sentries came forward. One of them paused to blow a whistle. The soldier in the tower looked down.

"Give us some light here!" the sentry said. Acknowledging the request with a wave, the soldier turned his spotlight away from the aerodrome and onto the field.

Right smack on Livingston.

Chapter Thirteen

"There's someone else down there!"

The sentries stopped when the soldier in the tower called down to them. They fingered their rifles nervously.

"Who is it?" one of them asked Colon. "Who else is out there?"

The private turned. "Well, Sergeant? Who are you?"

Livingston was lying behind his rifle. "I'm the guy who's going to pick off the soldier in the tower. You two take the others."

Colon smiled. An instant later, Livingston's rifle cracked; the tower guard flew backward, against the wall, and tumbled over. Concurrently, Colon leveled his own Karabiner and shot one of the sentries; in one swift motion, Lambert drew his knife and flung it underhand at the other guard, who also fell, his heart pierced.

Livingston scrambled up the ridge. When he arrived, Lambert said, "That was subtle. Now what?"

Lights in the other tower were turned on and a siren sounded. In the distance, engines were revved. In a few minutes, the field would be over-run by motorcycles.

Livingston started running to the tower. "Back to plan one," he yelled over his shoulder. "Up the legs and over the side."

Upon reaching the foot of tower, Livingston pushed his rifle through the barbed wire, then began shimmying up the leg of the tower. It was approximately twenty meters to the top; that part would be easy. Crossing the underbelly of the cabin to one of the other legs would not be. There were five slats, each a half meter apart, and from the ground there didn't appear to be much finger room atop each. But like everything else in the mission, it would have to do.

Lambert went up the pole behind Livingston, followed by Weyers. Colon stayed behind.

"Come on!" Livingston shouted back.

"You go! I'll cover you!"

"Forget it! They'll cut you to pieces!"

Colon remained at the base of the tower, looking back as headlights began appearing at the far side of the perimeter. Snorting with disgust, Livingston hurried up the strut and reached for the first of the horizontal beams.

"Dammit!"

"What's wrong?" Lambert asked.

"The thing's hammered so tight there's nothing to grip." He craned his head back. Reaching the wall of the cabin wasn't possible; the overhang was too great.

Plans. Even little ones were worthless. Livingston asked Colon to shine the flashlight on the underside of the cabin. He studied the strut.

Each leg was set in four blocks. He didn't know if there was time to do what he was planning, but he didn't have any other options. He told the others to get back down.

"What are you going to do?"

Livingston drew his knife. "Just get the hell down and stand back."

While Weyers and Lambert backed away, Livingston began prying at the blocks. He worked quickly, frantically, wedging the blade along the length of the first piece. The nails groaned and, slowly, the block began to come away.

Below, the other men drew their guns. Lambert guessed that they had two minutes at the most. Weyers concurred and made certain that everyone intended to fight rather than surrender. Colon raised his rifle, planning to pick off any German who came within range.

The first block thudded near Lambert's feet.

"Watch it, up there! You almost hit me!"

Atop the strut, Livingston feverishly dug the knife into the second block. He pushed his fingers beneath it, scraping his knuckles raw on the wound under the cabin, but he didn't stop. The second block came away, and he began on the third.

"You've got about a minute," Lambert yelled as the third block hit the ground near Weyers. But Livingston didn't have to work off the fourth one. His weight did the rest.

"Move back!" he shouted as the strut began to creak and groan. He wrapped his legs and arms around it as the fourth block popped off and the long, slender strut tore away from the cabin. It sagged slowly over the fence before snapping near the base. Livingston dropped the remaining three meters and landed on his back; he managed to roll aside just as the cabin crashed. Several large planks and beams pounded the sergeant.

The men wasted no time scurrying up the mound of rubble and over the fence.

Weyers was openly amazed as he hurried to Livingston's side. "Unbelievable!" he said as he pulled away the slats and helped the American to his feet. "That was the most incredible bit of engineering I've *ever* seen!"

"I think it was *un*engineering," Lambert said, "but whatever it was it was *merveilleux!*"

Livingston clutched his side and Weyers took his arm. "Are you all right?"

"I'll live."

Colon joined the group. "Fuck me," was all he said, grinning once at Livingston before starting across the compound.

Livingston urged the others to join him.

"Can you make it?" Weyers asked.

"Yes. Let's just *get going!*"

The trio started out and Livingston fell. Weyers stopped. "You probably cracked a rib—"

"Screw the rib, let's *go!*"

Livingston looked back. Outside the fence, motorcycles were roaring around the corner. To the right, several more were speeding toward them, across the aerodrome field. Colon dropped flat, ready to start firing. Lambert headed over. "I'm going to help Colon. You make for the airfield, *mes amis*. We'll hold them off as long as we can."

Livingston and Weyers started out again; after a few moments, Livingston fell to one knee.

"What's wrong?"

"Nothing, as long as I don't breathe. I'll be okay if I go slowly." Livingston looked up. "Don't *worry* about me. You just get upstairs and start dropping bombs!"

Weyers rose reluctantly. "I don't want to leave you."

Livingston snatched his pistol from its holster. "Get going, Weyers, or I swear I'll—"

The rest of the words were swallowed in an explosion that came from behind; a soldier had used a potato masher to tear a hole in the fence. A pair of motorcycles had already squeezed through and came roaring forward. Weyers reached for his gun and dropped to his belly, but before he could fire, the men on the bikes went down; behind them, a huge section of fence just seemed to vanish.

Chadli crowed with delight as he barreled through the barbed wire. Bullets ricocheted off the metal walls of the half-track, blasting away the distinctive swastika and palm-tree emblem on the door. The vehicle's headlights, which had been off, exploded. The Algerian returned the Germans' gunfire while Ogan, his face contorted with pain, held the steering wheel steady.

"Death to all conquerors!" Chadli shouted as he sprayed a line of bullets behind him, over the open carriage of the vehicle. Another motorcyclist fell. The rest held back and continued shooting at the half-track.

"I see Livingston . . . up ahead," Ogan rasped.

"I see them too," Chadli said as he took back the wheel. He leaned out the side and waved toward the two team members. "Come on! I have Ogan with me!"

Weyers and Livingston didn't move. The South African trained his gun on the Algerian.

"Don't!" Ogan yelled over the roar of the powerful Daimler engine. "It's all right!" He fell back against the seat, overtaxed by the exertion.

Weyers held his fire until he was certain that it was Ogan in the passenger's seat. When the half-track pulled alongside the two men, Weyers literally pushed Livingston on board, over the iron wall of the carriage.

The South African glowered at Chadli. "You worm! If you think this is going to make up for what you did—"

"I have many explanations to offer, Corporal Weyers," the Algerian said preemptorily, "but I will do so later. Just tell me, what is it that we need to do?"

"Pick up the others—there." Weyers pointed to the flashes of gunfire. "And then get to the planes. We need to reach one of the bombers."

Chadli scanned the airstrip. "I don't know bombers from mutton—"

"They're the big ones. I'll *show* you which. Just move it out."

Weyers was still on the tread guard when Chadli threw the half-track into gear and surged forward. The big man somersaulted in.

"Christ." He crawled next to Livingston. "Remind me never to insult a guy who's driving."

The sergeant patted him on the shoulder and leaned toward Ogan. "What are you doing here? You're in no condition to be playing hero."

"I . . . owe someone."

Livingston felt a jolt. "Who?"

Ogan spoke with effort. "Delphine. She . . . gave her life."

Livingston felt as though he'd been punched. Something else had obviously gone wrong, and this time it had cost them. But there was no time to mourn. Behind them, lights doused, the motorcycles began racing through the fence. The sergeant turned and crept slowly, painfully to the back of the carriage and began shooting. Because he couldn't see the enemy, he fired at the noise rising from their engines. He had no idea whether or not he hit anything but—from the sound, at least—no one seemed to be gaining on them.

Now and then, Livingston stole a look toward the distant hangars. From the amount of activity going on over there, an onlooker would have assumed that the invasion of North Africa was already under way. Spotlights searched the skies. Soldiers manned antiaircraft guns. But no one had lit the field, lest it make a clear target for Allied bombers. That, Livingston felt, gave them a chance.

Weyers knelt against the front of the carriage and fired over Chadli's head. The motorcyclists ahead of Colon and Lambert had stopped and doused their lights; no one was hitting anything in the dark, but everyone was afraid to move.

When the half-track came rocketing forward, Lambert looked back. Failing to recognize the vehicle in the dark, he prepared to shoot at it.

"Hold your fire, you bloody idiot!" Weyers screamed. "It's *us*!"

"*Zut!*"

The Frenchman scrambled to his feet and, with Colon, ran in a zigzag pattern toward the oncoming half-track. It slowed slightly and they hopped on board.

"Even Hedy Lamarr never looked so lovely!" Lambert gushed as he kissed the cold iron of the carriage.

Colon looked anxiously around the vehicle. "Where's Delphine?"

"Later!" Livingston yelled. "We've got a small army up our ass!"

Colon wriggled over. "Where *is* she, Sarge? Is she all right?"

Livingston dropped below the back wall while he fished the last magazine from his pouch. "I don't know how or why, Private, but she didn't make it. I'm sorry. I truly am."

There was a moment of silence, and then Colon seemed to explode. He began firing the Karabiner; somewhere in the distance a motorcycle screeched and fell. When the rifle was empty, Colon threw it from the truck and began shooting with his pistol.

In the flashes of gunfire, Livingston could see Colon's face. It was like looking into a nightmare.

Suddenly, Chadli shouted. "Look out in back!"

Livingston glanced up front as the half-track plowed through the line of soldiers who had been firing at them. The men scattered and regrouped, coming at the vehicle from both sides; several of them managed to get handholds. Weyers met one with a fist and sent him sprawling back; another jumped in and landed on Lambert. Two more stood on the tread guard and tried to get in, while a fifth man locked the crook of his elbow around Livingston's throat. Another drew his knife and wrestled with Chadli for the wheel.

With a howl of rage, Colon attacked the two men on the side. He shoved one back and pulled the other in, falling on the man and pummeling him with both fists. Cartilage cracked audibly and teeth were dislodged; yet with each piston-like blow it was Colon who cried, not the German.

Reaching behind him, Livingston managed to grab the hair of his attacker and pull him in. The man released his grip and lay awkwardly over the wall of the carriage. Livingston dispatched him with a karate blow to the neck, then darted to the cab and yanked the soldier away from Chadli. The German stumbled back, his pants leg catching in the massive treads. They dragged him under the half-track, his screams lost in the roar of the engine.

Livingston noticed Chadli holding his shoulder. "Are you all right?"

"Not . . . really."

The sergeant pulled the Algerian's hand back, saw a dark smear of blood.

"You opened the old wound. More over, I'll—"

"Grenade!"

Lambert's cry put all other concerns on hold. Livingston went over the wall, landing on top of Chadli and Ogan; everyone else flung themselves from the carriage. Moments later an explosion sent bent chunks of metal flying in all directions; the half-track plowed into a small Henschel biplane parked at the edge of the field, riding up the plane's tail and stopping at an incline.

Livingston sat up.

There was no one left in the carriage; there was barely even a carriage, all four walls having been blown out, huge slabs of the floor jutting up like splashes of liquid metal. Men lay scattered in the vehicle's wake. The lights of the pursuing motorcycles were still off, but Livingston could hear them coming near, saw their vague silhouettes against the horizon.

Holding his chest, he ran out and began kicking his men. All were dazed, but none seemed seriously hurt.

"Come on, you goddamn goldbricks!"

Lambert stirred. *"Dieu!* Can you believe that someone did that? Just pulled out a grenade—"

"I believe it! I *saw* it!" Livingston grabbed him. "Now gather the others and let's get the hell to a plane!"

Livingston snatched a pistol from an unconscious soldier and began firing at the motorcycles. By that time, his men were on their feet; so were many of the Germans, and two of them rushed at him. In the dark, still reeling, neither evidently saw that he had a gun. The sergeant shot them both, then followed the others toward the half-track. Weyers already had Ogan draped over his shoulders.

Livingston looked toward the line of aircraft on the runway. "Which one of the bombers should we make for?"

"We don't have much choice. The Heinkel is the only one that will carry us all."

"Good. Go there, I'll follow."

More soldiers were coming from the barracks—more than Livingston had expected to encounter. He turned as Chadli backed the half-track down off the biplane.

"You go too, Livingston."

"What are you going to do?"

"Don't worry about me. Just give me matches."

"*Why?*"

"Please—the matches!"

Livingston fished them from his pocket and flipped them to Chadli. The Algerian smiled.

"My family is safe because of you, Livingston. I owe you . . . more than I can ever repay. This, at least, is something."

"What is? Chadli, what are you going to do?"

Instead of answering, the Algerian turned the vehicle toward the barracks. As he drove, he unscrewed the top of the petrol tank strapped to the chassis beside the door. Bullets crashed through the windshield, and pressed Chadli, screaming, to the seat. But he didn't take his foot from the gas pedal.

Livingston had already begun to run after his comrades; Chadli's cry pulled him around. He watched as the Algerian managed to scrape the match—against his palm, it seemed—then slumped against the door and dropped the match down the spout.

The half-track exploded violently.

Chapter Fourteen

Livingston hit the dirt but continued to scrabble ahead. The heat of the fireball baked the back of his neck, and when it passed, he jumped to his feet. Bent with pain, he ran after the others. Shouts from behind indicated that casualties among the Wehrmacht defenders had been heavy.

The men paused behind a row of oil drums. The planes were a few hundred meters away, the giant Heinkel fourth in the row of over a dozen bombers. They were now clearly visible in the light of the burning half-track.

So, too, were the guards. Peering over the top of the drums, Livingston counted over twenty soldiers. They clearly intended to stand by the planes regardless of what emergency arose elsewhere.

"And just how did Escott expect us to rig dynamite with all those guards standing around?"

"There wouldn't be so many guards if Chadli hadn't turned us in," Weyers pointed out.

"Forget Chadli," Livingston said. "He did okay for us." He slipped back down, pressing his side. "The question now is how to get over there."

"The plane's got three guns," Weyers said. "If I

could reach it with someone else, I could start the plane while the extra man uses the starboard gun to cover the others."

"Colon's still dressed for the occasion," Livingston said. "Maybe he can walk you over." He glanced at the private. "Colon, are you okay?"

The soldier still looked as though he could kill with his teeth. He nodded once.

"Are you okay enough to walk over and sweet-talk your way into the plane?"

"Do I get to shoot the scum later?"

"If you have to."

"Then I'm okay."

Livingston faced the others. "Anyone still have a gun?"

"I do." Lambert pulled one from the stash of his robe. "There are only three or four shots left—"

"That's okay. Colon shouldn't need any at all. He'll take Weyers over at gunpoint, then tell the guards his prisoner planted dynamite and is going to show him where it is."

"Then we just walk in and Colon hits the upper turret," Weyers said.

"You've got it. It's just simple enough to work."

Weyers rubbed his big hands together. Colon took the gun from Lambert. "Remember," the South African said, "I'm on your side. Don't go shooting me in a fit of enthusiasm."

The men began marching over, Weyers's arms raised, Colon pushing him as they walked. When they were gone, Lambert slid over to Ogan's side. The Englishman's eyes were shut, and Lambert tapped his cheeks.

"Are you all right?" Lambert asked.

Ogan nodded weakly.

"We're going to get you out of here, Sergeant— to a real doctor. You don't know how lucky you are to be alive. Sergeant Livingston knows as much about medicine as he does about the sex life of the Führer."

The American ignored the quip; he was too busy watching Colon and Weyers as they made their way toward the airplane.

Colon didn't see Weyers or the plane. He wasn't thinking about the machine gun pointing from the open side of the dome behind the cockpit. The only thing on his mind was the soldier marching by the tail of the aircraft. The young soldier withdrew a flashlight as they approached.

The young German soldier. A brother to the bastards who had murdered Delphine.

The guard shined the beam on the newcomers. "Identify yourselves!"

Colon glowered from beneath his hooded brow. The gun felt hot in his hand, like it was a part of him.

Someone like this man murdered Delphine.

Weyers hissed from the side of his mouth. *"Answer him!"*

The private ground his teeth. His finger closed on the trigger.

"I said identify yourself!"

From the corner of his eye, Colon saw the machine gun up above. He *could* do a lot of damage with that. Slowly, he released his hold on the trigger. "I am *Panzergrenadier* Hans von Varest," he said quietly. "In exchange for his life, this saboteur has agreed to show me where he has planted dynamite and a timing device on the bomber."

"Dynamite?" The surprised guard studied both men in the light. "When did he go aboard?"

Colon repeated the question in English.

"This morning," Weyers answered. "While the sentry was peeing."

Colon translated and the guard snickered. "He wouldn't have gotten this far on *my* shift." He waved the flashlight once and resumed his march. "Go ahead, but be careful. With all that's going on here, he may try to get away and trigger the explosives himself."

"I know how to do my job," Colon replied.

By the time they reached wing, Weyers was livid. "I sweated a creek back there!" he said through his teeth. "Was that last gibe *really* necessary? And why the bloody hell did you wait so long to answer him in the first place?"

"I was trying to imagine how he'd look with a hole in his fucking head."

"Great. I'm getting into bed with a psychopath."

The guard looked over and Weyers fell silent. He stood back, hands still upraised, and nodded toward the turret. "The explosives are in there," he said, "just under the starboard gun."

Colon looked up. He frowned. "It's dark as a rat's ass up there. How'd you expect me to see a stinkin' thing?"

"What do you have to see? Just feel your way around."

The private called back to the sentry. "Would you throw me your light? I seem to have forgotten mine."

The guard came over and handed him the flashlight. "Forgotten your light? I thought you knew how to do your job, *kamerad*!"

Colon fired him a look, then relaxed. He could wait another few seconds.

The sentry returned to his post and, still holding his gun on Weyers, Colon ducked under the belly of the plane. He undid the latch and the forward entry hatch swung down. Colon motioned for Weyers to enter. He noticed the sentry shift uneasily. "Give us one minute," he told the German. "If this fool tries anything, shoot him."

As soon as they were inside, Colon tucked the gun in his belt and, snuggling past the oxygen tanks and thermos bottles strapped to the wall, he climbed into the turret.

"Well?" the guard shouted.

In the dull glow of the flashlight, Colon did a quick study of the gun. The maintenance crews hadn't gotten to this one yet; it was still covered with dust from a recent desert run, and the ammunition belts were just where the gunner had left them—loaded and ready to fire.

Colon doused the light and dropped it to Weyers.

"What's wrong?" asked the guard. "Did the light die?"

In the darkness, Colon noted the positions of the nearest sentries. He swung the machine gun around, aimed it down.

"No, not *it*—*you*, you bloody damn Kraut!"

Colon opened fire. Like a top, the guard whirled under the impact of bullets designed to rip apart the metal shell of an airplane. The private swung to the other side and gunned down two other men. Then, while Weyers slid into the pilot's seat, Colon turned to cover the approach of his teammates.

Livingston moved out with the first report, which had come none too soon. Realizing that only a handful of men had infiltrated the base, and that their target was not the antiaircraft guns, the German soldiers had begun withdrawing from the perimeter and were closing in on the airstrip.

With Ogan in his arms, Livingston ran toward

the plane, Lambert bringing up the rear. Twice, Lambert had to rush ahead to help Livingston when he buckled and fell to one knee under the weight and pain.

They arrived just as Weyers fired up the first of the two huge propellers. Lambert climbed in and helped Livingston get Ogan aboard. They sat the sergeant major in the radio operator's seat, lashing him securely with the shoulder harness. Both men went quickly to the cockpit while, above them, the machine gun chattered.

"It sounds as though Colon is having a rewarding cultural exchange with the Nazis," Lambert said.

The second propeller spit, clattered, then roared to life. The cockpit shook and filled with the overpowering smell of high-octane fuel.

Livingston sat heavily in the copilot's seat. "Where do you want us?" He had to shout to be heard.

"Put Lambert on the nose guns, in case the Jerries scramble fighters. The guns are forward, in the bombardier's compartment."

Lambert looked around, saw a short, sloping corridor to the right of the pilot's seat. "Down there?"

Weyers nodded and, throwing the men a thumbs-up, Lambert disappeared down the passageway.

"What about me?" Livingston asked.

"I'll need you to be bombardier, but first I need something else. Maintenance never got to this aircraft after the day's run. You have to go below."

"And do what?"

Weyers flashed a mirthless grin. "See if there are any bombs on this crate."

* * *

Weyers admitted that somewhere, among the myriad controls, there had to be a bomb indicator. "But I don't know where it is, and I don't have time to search. And at the rate Colon's pissing ammunition, we'll be dry in a few minutes. We damn well better be ready to take off then."

Livingston slid from his seat. "Where's the bomb bay?"

"Straight through that door." He gestured behind him, then handed Livingston the sentry's flashlight. "You passed the bomb racks after you dropped off Ogan."

The sergeant felt queasy; he was certain that even in the dark, he'd have noticed bombs lining the walls. Despite the pain in his chest, he hurried through the door into the small, stuffy bomb bay.

The flashlight beam played across the bomb hoist bracket, then up and down the walls. He found the bomb bay light in the rear, turned it on, looked through the small room.

His heart sank.

Instead of the stacks of bombs that he'd hoped to find, Livingston saw only three. They were piled like a stubby L, and he judged them to weigh roughly five hundred pounds each. But under the circumstances, they seemed small. Woefully small.

He ran back to report to Weyers.

"Three, is it? Well, then, you'll just have to make them count."

"I've never done this before," Livingston said, his manner calm, pragmatic. "Any suggestions?"

"I've never done it before either," Weyers said as he looked for the fuel gauge. "When you go down there, just do two things: Use the bombsight . . . and pray."

Livingston peered out the window, a huge hemisphere of glass that comprised the entire front of the aircraft. "Apart from the bombs, is there anything else we have to worry about?"

"Truthfully? This plane is my idea of hell, Sergeant. I don't know what half of this stuff does."

"What about the half we need to fly? *Can you get us off the ground?*"

I think so. If not"—he looked out the side, at the darkened row of aircraft—"not having enough bombs won't be a problem. We'll just plow into these sitting ducks."

"If we're taking a vote, I'd prefer to die of old age." Lambert piped up.

"I'm with Lambert," Livingston said. "Just do your best, and do it fast." He thought he saw soldiers moving on the adjoining strip, where the fighters were lined up; in the dark, he couldn't be certain. "Lambert, are you ready down there? We may have company."

"I see them," he shouted back. "Don't worry, I'm a terrible host."

Dust burned off the engines as they heated, clouds of fine powder swirling past the windows. Weyers squinted at the gauges. He hadn't turned on the cockpit light so they wouldn't be targets; even though the dials were luminous, they were difficult to read. "Engine pressure . . . looks good. Flap position . . . right. There's the air speed indicator. . . ." He took a deep breath and gripped the handles of the control yoke. "To hell with it. Let's go."

Weyers throttled up; the engines roared; the bomber stood still.

"What is it?" Livingston demanded.

The South African shook his head. "I don't understand. We've got the—" He bit off the rest of the sentence. "Bloody hell."

"What?"

"The blocks."

"What?"

"The bloody *wheel* blocks!"

Livingston punched his palm. "Jesus! Can one person move them?"

"If he's Captain Marvel, sure. Otherwise—in the dark, under fire, it'd be impossible." He pushed the engines to the maximum. "All we can do is try to roll over them."

The twin propellers screamed, their droning louder than the ever present crack of Colon's machine gun. The cockpit eased up as the two front wheels, each the size of a man, strained against the fat wedges of wood. Suddenly, the plane lurched up and over them. It thumped down hard, and Weyers quickly steered onto the strip.

"A little *smoother* next time, Monsieur Pilot!" Lambert said. His gun chattered and the cockpit filled with a deafening roar. "*Regardez!* They're coming to give you flying instructions!"

The German assault was at once the bravest and most foolhardy thing Livingston had ever seen. A company of soldiers took up positions on the airstrip and began firing at them: seven men against an onrushing bomber. Lambert cut them down before they could do any damage. But their action underscored the fact that the war was going to be a long one; there was no way that men like these would ever surrender. Hostilities would last until Hitler literally ran out of Germans.

The aircraft picked up speed as it taxied. Behind them, on the adjoining runway, Livingston could see black clouds of smoke billow from the engines of the cannon-armed Messerschmitts.

"They're coming after us," Livingston said.

"They'll probably get in the air before us, too,"

Weyers complained. "I don't know what the air speed is for this tub, but they built the runway this long for a reason."

The bomber was halfway down the strip when the first of the fighters began to taxi.

"Rotter!" Weyers called down. "Can you do anything to delay them port-side?"

"*Rien.* I have zero horizontal play."

Weyers tried the intercom. Colon wasn't wearing his headset, and the pilot flung his own unit aside. "Bloody unprofessionals!" he murmured as he looked for the horizontal stabilizer trim switch. He pulled a lever, activated the cockpit ventilation system, swore at the burst of warm air, and finally found the right switch.

But if the private wasn't wearing his headset, he *was* watching the Messerschmitts. And as Livingston looked on, the first of the nimble fighters had its tires shot out and collapsed on its underbelly. The sergeant rattled his fist in triumph. Both tires were hooded with metal, only their bottom third showing; it was an incredible bit of marksmanship. The fighter skidded ahead in a wild, smoky spin and blocked the runway.

"Nice job," Weyers muttered as he concentrated on the rapidly dwindling runway. There was no more time to delay and, muttering a prayer, he pulled back on the controls.

The plane rose heavily but steadily. Weyers immediately banked toward the harbor.

"Thank the Good Lord," he murmured.

"It wasn't God, it was you," Livingston said. "God was too busy helping Colon."

"Let's hope He's got enough time left for you," Weyers said as he wiped his forehead. "If we drop our load on the airfield, they can still use the desert to takeoff. It'll be bumpy, but they can do it."

"And if we only hit a few fighters, they'll have enough left to strafe the beaches."

"Right-o. Likewise the antiaircraft guns. So I suggest we go after the bombers. With any luck, we'll hit one that's been serviced—"

"—and loaded with bombs. Chain reaction."

Weyers nodded as he turned the plane around. "Remember, you're not only going to have to eyeball it, but also you'll have to drop them on the first pass. With all that artillery they've got, we won't get a second chance."

Livingston swung to his right and backed down the slanting accessway.

"*Bonjour!*" Lambert said. The Frenchman was sitting on the spare leather seat, his hands on the chin turret controller. Livingston curled up on the floor, to his left, and peered through the bombsight. There were two overlapping images; he twisted a knob on the side until they came into focus. One hand remained on the knob, ready to make minor adjustments as they descended.

"This is it, Sergeant!" Weyers shouted down. "You've got about thirty seconds until we're over our target!"

Livingston examined the glowing dials of the control panel on the wall. He threw the bomb-arming switch; a light went on. He looked down at three levers jutting from the floor.

"Weyers! Everything's labeled but some handles. Any idea what they do?"

"How many are there?"

"Three."

"The one nearest you *should* open the bomb door."

"If it doesn't?"

"Then it's the bomb-release lever, and you'll probably blow us out of the sky."

Livingston grabbed the knob on top of the nearest lever. When he was growing up, he used to have one friend, a rabbi's son. The boy often talked about feeling something in the *kishkes*, a place in the gut that knew more than the brain and felt more than the soul. For the first time in his life, Livingston felt something in the *kishkes*.

Fear and exhilaration.

"The Lady or the Tiger," he said under his breath as he pushed the lever forward. Even in the dark, he saw Lambert's eyes go wide.

The plane rattled. Gears ground.

After a long moment, a panel light went on: The doors were open.

Lambert exhaled loudly. "*Alors*. Having two women in a tub is *not* the greatest joy a man can know."

Livingston said he hoped to make the comparison one day. At the moment, he wasn't confident about his chances. The aircraft rattled more violently than before as Weyers began his pass over the base. A real pilot would never have risked putting the bomber into a power dive this low, but Weyer's didn't know it couldn't be done, and so he did it.

Flak exploded around them. Fortunately, Livingston realized, they were all bursts from the smaller, seaward-facing guns; the larger ones had not yet been turned around.

Despite the din, Livingston heard something drop behind him. He glanced back and was surprised to see Colon. Flak must have burst the turret glass: there was blood on Colon's cheeks, his hair was blown straight back from the wind, and his face was nearly blue from the cold. He was hugging himself to get warm. He must have come down from the turret and was thrown from the cockpit by the steep descent of the plane.

The sergeant turned back to the bombsight. He swung his feet around, used them to keep from sliding forward. He kept his right hand on the bombsight knob and his left hand on the middle lever. He'd throw this one to drop the first bomb, then use the other to release the remaining pair.

"Ready to level off! Holler when you let them go, so I can pull out!" Weyers yelled.

Livingston felt the nose come up. There was no light below, just the black, indistinct shapes of the bombers. Beside him, Lambert fired down at anti-aircraft guns on the port side. Livingston was surprisingly calm as he pushed the levers in turn.

"Now!"

The nose of the bomber continued to rise and then pivot as Weyers banked to the south. Livingston pulled himself to the window and watched anxiously for the explosions. He felt a sense of despair as the first small blast fell short of any bombers. The second hit a plane, destroying it, but the explosion he'd hoped for didn't come.

Then the third bomb hit. One of the bombers exploded violently; moments later, a wall of fire lifted the entire line of planes into the air. The aircraft returned to the earth in countless pieces, tumbling as though they were moving in slow motion; as they rained down, balls of flame from erupting bombs rolled across the field to the second strip, setting many of the fighters aflame.

Bodies lay strewn about the field. Those who could run or crawl headed away from the landing strips. The antiaircraft guns were barking, but there were far fewer than before as flames chased the gunners back. Very few bursts came close to the fleeing bomber.

Lambert threw his head back and laughed. Above, Weyers cheered. Colon wriggled over and Livingston looked back at him; both men smiled and Colon extended his bloody hand.

"Fuck me!" Colon said.

Livingston grinned. For once, they had no disagreement about what had just transpired. None at all.

Chapter Fifteen

The starboard propeller barked just before Weyers did.

"Bad news, mates."

Livingston had been sitting beside the unconscious Ogan, redressing his wounds. Crouched beneath spare oxygen tanks, he hobbled over. Lambert, looking incongruous in his dirty robe, had been trying to coax a coffee maker into operation; he gave it up and followed Livingston to the cockpit. Colon had remained below, at the nose gun.

The cabin was cold, the location of the heater a mystery, and when the men spoke, their breath came in vaporous puffs.

"What's wrong?" Livingston asked.

"You know how we were complaining about the maintenance they didn't do on this ship?"

"Yes."

"Well, there's something else the blighters never did. They never gave us any fuel."

Livingston shook his head. A hop to Gibraltar. Linking up with the Royal Navy. A ticket home. More useless plans.

"No bombs, no fuel, no coffee," Lambert complained. "What kind of a war is this, anyway?"

"How much farther can we go?" Livingston asked.

In response, the port propeller coughed, then the starboard engine sputtered again.

"The truth is, Sergeant, I've got to think about setting her down *now*. Otherwise, she'll be picking her own time and place."

Both engines rattled again. Livingston sat in the co-pilot's chair. They'd been aloft for just over an hour, heading due west. It was dark and cloudy and they had no idea where they were, save that they were seven thousand feet above Algeria, probably near the Moroccan border.

"Pick up anything on the radio?"

Weyers shook his head. "It's quiet and dark out there. No one wants to make themselves a target."

"So we can't even find a nice little town to set ourselves down."

The engine kicked on one side, then the other. Weyers began to nose downward.

"Hell, Sergeant, I can't even promise we'll set down on land. We may have gone far enough to be over the Mediterranean by now."

"Better the sea than the mountains," Lambert said.

Weyers stole a look at the others. His expression told Livingston that he couldn't guarantee they wouldn't hit the side of a mountain either. The cockpit seemed to grow even colder.

The altimeter was spinning counterclockwise. Weyers licked his lips. He hit the landing gear and there was a grinding of machinery; the "down" light flashed.

"Thank God for that much," Lambert sighed.

The engines were coughing steadily now, and

each time they did, the plane dipped to the opposite side. At last, a red warning light came on: They were nearly out of fuel.

"Aren't we falling a little fast?" Lambert asked.

Weyers nodded. "I want to get down as quickly as possible . . . save fuel so we've a little extra time to pick a landing site."

Lambert slid into the flight officer's seat and buckled in. Livingston did up his own harness, then called down to Colon to do likewise. The plane began to whistle as it descended. Livingston put his face to the window, cupped his hands on either side.

They plummeted into clouds and emerged a few seconds later. It was still utterly black, without a hint of what might lie ahead.

Suddenly, Livingston shouted. "Get her up! *Fast!*"

Weyers responded reflexively, using the flaps and the plane's last stores of fuel to bring the nose up. He noticed, as they passed over head, the factory smokestacks he'd narrowly avoided.

He exhaled loudly just as both engines clattered their death throes. Weyers leveled the bomber off. "This is it, mates. Now it's in the lap of the gods."

There was a wild drumming on the underbelly of the plane as they passed over what sounded like a row of trees. Metal groaned; Livingston didn't even want to think about what was happening to the landing gear.

Suddenly, the pounding stopped. So did the plane; it slowed abruptly, stood on its nose, hung upright for an instant, then crashed over.

The initial impact threw Livingston against the straps and all but cut off his breath. Upside down, he struggled to undo them, his face pounding as blood rushed to his head. Something sloshed; he had no idea whether it was inside his ears or inside the cockpit.

Livingston slipped his arms from the harness and tumbled out. He gasped for air as he landed on the roof of the cockpit. His chest felt as though there was a knife in it, but that wasn't his greatest concern. The windshield had cracked somewhere and there was foul-smelling water at his feet. The cockpit was filling quickly. He had no idea whether or not they were on fire, though at least there was nothing on board that could explode.

Colon dropped down from the overturned gun. "Is everyone all right?"

"I'm okay," Livingston answered. No one else spoke. "Go back and see about Ogan. I'll take care of these two."

The plane groaned and settled farther on its back. Livingston felt around, touched someone's hand. It was tacky and warm. Blood. He reached up and undid the seatbelt, caught Lambert as he dropped. After propping him against a control panel, Livingston felt his way forward, sloshing through water that was already up to his knees. He reached Weyers, and the South African began to moan.

"Wh—who hit me?"

"Don't worry about it now," Livingston said as he opened the harness. "We've got to get out of here."

The big man dropped down and Livingston slid a shoulder under his arm. Gritting his teeth against the pain, the sergeant walked him to the fuselage, where Colon was just kicking out a window.

"Door's blocked," he explained. "You'll have to feed the guys to me."

Livingston walked over. The tart odor was stronger here. "What are we in, some kind of swamp?"

Colon nodded. "Can't see nothin' out there but trees and water."

"It figures," Livingston said as Colon squeezed out.

When they'd passed the three men from the bomber, Colon and Livingston slogged once around the aircraft to make certain there were no fires on board. Then they sat down on the reedy shore.

As best as they could determine, neither Weyers nor Lambert was seriously wounded. A few of the cuts on Lambert's chest had split because of the harness; otherwise, he seemed fine. Weyers had suffered cuts on his face and arm when the windshield shattered, but he, too, was all right. Both were fully conscious now and grumbling about the stench.

Feeling more drained than he ever had been, Livingston didn't care where they were. Colon was already laying back on the rank earth; Livingston shut his eyes and joined him.

And leapt up moments later as something warm, soft, and wet brushed his forehead.

Major General Patton had just finished jogging in place when there was a knock at the door. Panting, he sat behind his desk.

"Come in!"

Two men entered and saluted, An orderly shut the door behind them and Patton's sallow face took on a vibrant glow.

"Sergeant Major Ogan. Sergeant Livingston. A pleasure. Truly a pleasure to meet you two."

He rose, returned their salutes, and offered

them chairs. Livingston went quickly to his, Ogan more slowly.

"How're you both feeling?"

"A little like Lazarus, sir," Livingston said. "But all things considered, we're not bad off."

"Better Lazarus than St. Peter." Patton regarded Livingston. "Sergeant, I understand you found a form of life lower than the enemy."

It took him a moment to understand what the officer meant. When he did, he grinned. "Yes, sir. If I never see a camel again, I'll die a happy man."

"You're lucky those people didn't blow your goddamn brains out instead of helping you. They thought you were Germans trying to blow up the plants because they had sold iron to the Allies."

"We're lucky, sir, that when the camels came over and licked us, I swore in English and another of our men swore in French."

Patton glanced at a paper on his desk. "That would be . . . Lambert."

"Yes, sir."

The major general snorted. "It's about time the French did our boys some good. Those sons of bitches actually fought *against* us when we hit Algiers. They were afraid the Germans would win and then kick their cans if they joined us."

"I can't answer for other Frenchmen, but Lambert did a *lot* of good, sir. Everyone on the team did."

The phone rang, and while Patton took the call, Livingston sat back in the thickly cushioned chair.

Livingston still couldn't believe that it was over, that they were about to be shipped back home. From the moment they crashed in Mar Chico, a small lagoon in the provincial capital of Nador, until the time they reached Casablanca a week later, it was as though there was no end to the struggling: for food, for shelter, for clothing, for transportation. Three of those days had been spent in Nador itself while Ogan regained his strength; the other four consisted of a camel caravan in which the men traveled slowly southwest. They paid their way by caring for the animals and standing watch while the merchants rested.

All the while, they had no information about what had happened when the Allies hit Algiers, Oran, and Casablanca. Dressed in Arab clothes, they spoke to people only when they had to, and avoided villages unless they needed supplies.

After leaving the caravan in Rabat, the group walked the remaining eighty kilometers to Casablanca. They were nearly crawling when they spotted an American sentry standing beneath an American flag at a bus terminal off the Place Mirabeau in the eastern outskirts of the city. Dragging himself over, Livingston asked what had happened to the invasion forces.

The soldier looked the listing, grizzled figure up and down. As though reciting from a manual, he said in a stilted monotone, "I'm sorry, but we're not permitted to converse with local—"

Livingston grabbed his lapels. "I'm an American sergeant on special assignment, soldier, and you'll tell me what happened or I'll shove your head so far up your ass it'll be right back on your goddamn shoulders!"

The soldier told him.

Major General Patton had taken Casablanca with ease. The landing at Oran was accomplished with great loss of life but was successful. And the assault on Algiers had been the most difficult of all.

Livingston tensed as the soldier related what had happened.

"Resistance was fierce, and two destroyers were lost. But for some reason, the Germans didn't hit us with very much air power. It's doubtful we could have taken the city if they had."

Smiling, Livingston collapsed in the soldier's arms.

That was three days ago.

Livingston spent the next two days in the local hospital, recuperating from what he learned were two broken ribs. The five team members shared the same ward, but they spoke little. Ogan fought a fever, Lambert winked at the nurses, Weyers read airplane manuals, and Colon listened to the radio and slept. For the most part, Livingston just lay on his back, staring at the white ceiling and savoring their triumph.

And life. Savoring it in his *kishkes*.

Patton hung up the phone. "They're ready for you, gentlemen. I think you'll find this plane somewhat more comfortable than the one you flew in on." He came around the desk and offered his hand to each man in turn. "Have a pleasant trip and thanks for coming. I'm glad I had this chance to meet you both and offer my thanks and personal congratulations for a job brilliantly done."

Livingston was moved. More than that, he was proud—proud of a group of cocky individualists who had somehow managed to work together as a unit. He'd miss them—even the stuffed shirt Ogan who, since he'd regained consciousness in the hospital, hadn't said more than two words to his teammates. But he had the will of a lion, something Livingston couldn't help but admire.

He also, clearly, was a man with something on his mind.

On the ride to the makeshift airfield where the

other team members would be waiting, Ogan sat stiffly, staring down at his lap.

"Nice uniforms they dug up," Livingston said, brushing lint from his trousers as the jeep rolled south along the wide Boulevard Abdelmoumen. Ogan continued to stare at the squat, white buildings racing by, their facades gleaming in the bright sunlight. "Patton probably would have blown a gasket if we'd gone to see him in someone's borrowed civvies. My guess is they'll ask for them back, though."

Ogan said nothing, but Livingston wasn't really surprised. The sergeant major didn't seem to have room in his skull for anything except Barker, regulations, and probably Barker's family and friends.

Then Ogan surprised him. Turning slowly from the window, he said, "Sergeant—soon to be lieutenant, I'm sure—I want you to know that my own sentiments echo those of the major general. You did a smashing job."

"Like I said, we all did."

"No, that's not quite true. I jeopardized the mission several times, both from inexperience and . . . for my own reasons."

"To protect Barker? Those were understandable reasons."

"Understandable, perhaps. Acceptable, no. I loved Harold Barker, and that love clouded my decisions." He touched his chest. "*I* know, in here, that I was not fit to command."

Livingston began to protest, but Ogan held up his hand.

"Save your breath, Livingston. We both saw who it was that Patton talked to in there. Now I wish to formalize what we already know."

His movements stiff and pained, Ogan reached

into his jacket pocket and withdrew a folded piece of paper. He handed it to Livingston. "This is a trifle unorthodox, I'll admit, but then so was this entire operation. I want you to read this ... to *have* it. I want it to *stick*."

Livingston scanned the one-paragraph document. When he was finished, he blurted out, "This is ridiculous. You can't just name me leader after the fact."

Ogan smiled a rare half smile. "I know. And frankly, I'm not sure what headquarters will have to say about it. Now that our task is through, I suppose it's all rather academic. But man to man, on the record or off, I want you to know how I feel. You saved my life, and you made certain that Barker didn't give *his* life in vain. That's helped me deal with his death. What I've done is a small thing ... a *very* small thing compared to that."

Livingston was caught completely off guard. He didn't know whether Ogan had really changed or if he himself had seriously misjudged him; a little of both, he decided. And as they pulled onto the airstrip where the other members of the Force Five team were already gathered, he was genuinely sorry that he wouldn't get the chance to serve with Ogan again.

He had a feeling the man would be as true a friend as any who ever lived.

Epilogue

The men sat around a large table in a small room in Washington. There were maps spread before them, and a pair of dossiers.

The maps were of Russia, mostly of Stalingrad and the surrounding regions.

A tired-looking General George Marshall sat between two other officers; across from him were the pallid British Ambassador to the United States, Lord Hugo Ball, and General L. M. Beebe of Military Operations.

Marshall dug the heels of his hands into his eyes. "I just can't go along with this. For one thing, I don't want Donovan and his OSS people chewing me out again for sending soldiers into their territory. For another, I just don't see why the Russians can't save *themselves*! What are you asking me to send men into, gentlemen? A nursery?"

"It isn't a matter of the Russians being *unable* to save themselves." said the slender, ashen Ball. He coughed into the back of his hand, obviously unsettled by the general's resistance. "It's a matter of priorities. The Russians in Stalingrad are

spread so thin they're afraid that if they give anywhere, the Germans will take the city."

"The Russians have got *four* armies headed
there! Freeing up a company or two to attack a
few supply frigates shouldn't compromise them
that much."

"We think it might," Ball replied. "Don't mis-
understand. The Russians are a brave people, especially when it comes to defending their
homeland. But they function best using brute
force, and that's not what we need here. We need
men who understand mobility, stealth, and discre-
tion."

"You need *lunatics*! What you're proposing is a
suicide mission. I went along with Whitehall on
the Algerian team because the president wanted
to show Churchill that we're behind him. But this!
I'd rather shoot the men myself and be merciful.
And to do it for the Russians, who would *still* be
on the sidelines if Hitler hadn't invaded—it's
damn near vulgar."

The elderly British general spoke up. "That may
well be, but there's another matter to consider."

"Which is?"

"Even if the Russians were to spare personnel,
we're not sure we *want* them to have what's going
to be on those boats."

Marshall sat back. He steepled his hands,
tapped the fingers together, "Now we get to it.
What's going on, gentlemen? What have you been
holding back?"

"Simply that we believe there will be more than
just supplies in that shipment. There's cargo
which the Communists could one day use to their
advantage."

"Specifically?"

Beebe briefed Marshall. The general was suddenly wide awake.

"Are you sure about that?"

"Quite," Ball said. "So you see, there really is something to be gained here if you let us hold on to your two men just a bit longer." He folded his hands on the table. "I appreciate that the OSS gave you a bit of a talking to. Frankly, I understand their position. The Algerian thing would have been a joint operation between Donovan's boys and British intelligence if there hadn't been that leak in the SIS. But the army team did so well that our own three charges are going to be asked back . . . and we have a feeling they won't be as effective without *your* boys."

Marshall turned to the dossiers. There were two of them, each stamped in red: "Eyes Only" and "Force Five."

"Livingston and Colon," the general said, paging through the files. "A commendation from Patton. Recommendations for promotions." He rubbed his eyes again. "What a waste of fine men this will be. But we've spent enough time on this part of the agenda. Gentlemen, the team is yours."

Marshall slapped the files shut. As the Englishmen turned to a proposed tour of North Africa by President Roosevelt, the chief of staff took some solace in the fact that if anyone looked like they knew what they were doing, it was the Force Five bunch.

God help them, he thought as an aide handed him another file. *This time they'll need it.*

Watch for

Destination: Stalingrad

next in the Force Five *series*
coming soon from Lynx